Karen Jennings

Finding Soutbek

Holland Park Press London

Published by Holland Park Press 2012

Copyright © Karen Jennings 2012

First Edition

The moral right of Karen Jennings to be identified as the author of this work has been asserted by her in accordance with the Copyright, Designs and Patents Act of 1988.

All rights reserved. Without limiting the rights under the copyright reserved above, no part of this publication may be reproduced, stored in a retrieval system or transmitted in any form or by any means, electronic, mechanical, photocopying, recording or otherwise, without the prior permission of both the copyright owner and Holland Park Press.

A CIP catalogue record for this book is available from The British Library.

ISBN 978-1-907320-20-0

Cover designed by Reactive Graphics

Printed and bound by CPI Group (UK) Ltd, Croydon, CR0 4YY

www.hollandparkpress.co.uk

The focal point of the novel is the small town of Soutbek. Its troubles, hardships and corruption, but also its kindness, strong community and friendships, are introduced to us in a series of stories about intriguingly interlinked relationships.

Contemporary Soutbek is still a divided town – the upper town destitute, and the lower town rich, largely ignorant – and through a series of vivid scenes, the troubled relationship between Pieter Fortuin, the town's first coloured mayor, and his wife Anna is revealed.

In so many ways the past casts a long shadow over the present, not in the least through the unreliable diaries of Pieter van Meerman promoted by Pieter Fortuin and Professor Pearson, a retired white historian. They give us a unique insight into the lives of the seventeenth-century Dutch explorers, and hint at a utopian society, suggesting that Soutbek is the birthplace of assimilation and integration.

The blossoming friendship between Anna, Sara, a foundling, and Willem, Pieter Fortuin's nephew, is unsettled by David, Anna's and Pieter's son. His father has bought David a bright future, but when he comes back from boarding school David appears alienated from his father and from his old friend, the former gardener Charles Geduld, just as Anna starts to accept him as her son.

Is there hope, or are we left with Willem's conclusion that 'he would spend the rest of his life working off the debt of his family's poverty'?

A wonderful, moving story that keeps you spellbound, yet also paints a thought-provoking picture of life in contemporary South Africa.

For Carlo

And here stands man, stripped of myth, eternally starving, surrounded by every past there has ever been, digging and scrabbling for roots, even if he must dig for them in the most remote antiquities.

Nietzsche, *The Birth of Tragedy*

Those sitting on the shore, the elderly mostly, did not look back. They knew well enough what was behind them: the blaze working its way through the upper town, its flames burning high so that even down on the beach the heat could be felt on their backs. They looked out at the dark waves that glowed before them. They did not speak. They looked forward only, and waited.

Others, the young, who had no memory of past fires, stood in the bushes near the shore and called out to each other, pointing and whooping. They forgot that they were watching their homes burning. They thought simply of the spectacle, feeling excited. Around them dogs barked, running along the line of vegetation, or stood whimpering near their masters.

Others still, the mothers and fathers, walked away from the beach, into the low scrub of the flatlands. They searched for dry bushes or the dead branches of stunted trees, thinking about the nights to follow. They knew the cold that was to come, the homelessness and the cold, and so they fanned out; some returning to the beach, hopeful of driftwood.

Further inland the river, swollen by weeks of rain, had flooded, washing away bridges as it went. Its waters now covered vineyards and farmland, the roads were all mud. For those whose homes were burning there was no hope of being reached by the fire truck fifty kilometres away. Even the rain, which before had been so persistent, had stopped. They could only wait until the blaze had burned itself out, making do then with what remained.

To the west the lower town lay untouched by fire, its inhabitants asleep.

Outside it was dim, the sky lightening at the horizon and broadening over the waves. Already gulls were flying low, calling. The mayor rolled over in bed and pushed his face into the pillow, his knees brushing against those of his wife. He felt her body stiffen as he moved towards her and then the shifting of the bed as she turned from him, rising quietly, leaving the room. He did not lift his face from the pillow. He felt the warmth of his own breath on his nose and lips and went back to sleep.

When he woke again the day was light through the curtains. He stood slowly, placing each foot carefully on the ground. In the bathroom she had left the window open and the room was cool, his bare feet cold on the tiled floor. He went to the basin and ran the water until it was warm, washing his face and lathering it with shaving cream. Then he picked up his razor and slid it along his cheek, down to his jawline and below. There was no other noise in the house but for the razor on his face. He began again, further along his cheek, following a steady line. In the front room the phone began to ring. He stopped for a moment and listened, then putting down the razor, placed a hand on either side of the basin. He leaned heavily and sighed. Through the window came the smell of salt, of shrubs, and underneath, the thick smell of human filth. He cleared his throat, staring down into the white of the basin, his hands gripping its sides. When he looked up again he saw his face, grave in the mirror. To the left was the reflection of the open window, framing a small section of sea and sky. He looked at grey clouds, a grey sky. It was as though the world existed in that square alone. As though there were nothing else beyond the grey.

The houses of the lower town had been built on a steep sea-facing incline. Many were the holiday homes of farming or city families, but mostly the hill was dominated by retired couples come to live out their days with a sea view. Beyond, the hill flattened into shrublands, spreading out in long plains that touched mountains at the horizon. To the east, the lower town was flanked by a channel, dry since the 1920s when the river had chosen a different route to the sea. In the past elephants had lived there, rubbing smooth the rocks as they waded. Now the riverbed separated the lower from the upper town. Ending at high cliffs that overlooked the sea, the upper town had grown on flat land before sloping into a small bay where fishing boats mouldered on the shore. On the far edge of the bay stood the old fish factory, closed five years previously. Its long cement jetty, which had stretched out into the sea, now lay ruined; the uprights fallen into the waves below. The furthest section was still standing, and on it remained the height of a crane, its hook hanging like a gibbet.

Despite a week having passed since the fire, people were still living on the beach of the small bay, sleeping on newspapers and plastic bags. Cement-brick houses, built more than a decade before as part of a government scheme for reconstruction, now lay black and broken on the rise. For the rest, shacks were piles of burnt plastic and ash, indistinguishable from one another. Some inhabitants had returned, salvaging what they could from the rubble, moving into the deserted homes of others. They made roofs out of scorched zinc sheets, assembling their new homes amongst the piles of the old, using what remained. Many had taken what they could to the edges of the town, their homes spreading out onto the cliffs, held together by nothing. Parts of the upper town now lay uninhabited, left to the rummagings of dogs and rats. In the scattered landscape these heaps took on a sense of permanence.

Already complaints were coming to the mayor from the lower town: washing stolen from lines, tools and materials disappearing from garages, and worst of all, the smell of human faeces that made its way down with the breeze.

'Civilised people,' the mayor thought, 'would have some pride. Civilised people wouldn't live like that.'

Remaining before the mirror, he listened to the murmurs as the ringing phone was answered. Soon footsteps approached. He shifted so that he could see her in the mirror; part of her face, her shoulder.

'Yes?'

'It was Hannes Fouché from Doorn farm. He's found a girl. He wants to know if you'll come fetch her.'

He wiped his face, nodded. Then, abruptly, turning from the basin, he reached out to the window, pulling it closed.

Much of the morning had passed by the time he arrived at Doorn farm. A week of sun had done little to improve the mire of the yard. Empty fruit crates rested against a wall of the barn behind a small tractor with a red flag at its rear. To the right of the yard two large dogs, chained to a post, barked in the mayor's direction. He ignored them, looking down at his shoes in the mud as he walked to the house, trying to balance on his toes.

Hannes greeted him at the door, 'Morning, Mr Fortuin. How about some coffee for you?'

The mayor shook his head, said he had a lot to do. Hannes nodded his understanding and then pointed in the direction of the barn. 'I found her there early this morning. Drinking milk straight from the cow. I tried chasing her away, but she won't go.'

'Did she say anything?' the mayor asked.

'Nothing. Not a word. All I can think is the fire you folks had scared her and now she's lost.'

'Maybe. Where is she now?'

'I put her with the maid. Francine is away and can't get back until the roads are clear.'

'I see.'

The mayor walked round to the rear of the house and found the girl sitting on the kitchen step biting into a piece of bread. She was maybe fifteen or sixteen with short hair, unkempt, wearing a dress under a jersey that hung well past her hips. Her feet were bare. She chewed with her mouth open and did not look at the mayor when he spoke to her, asking her name. In her open mouth the teeth were small and yellow. A woman came from the kitchen and touched the girl's shoulder.

'Go with him,' she said. 'He will take care of you.'

The girl put the last piece of bread in her mouth, chewing slowly. When she had finished swallowing, she got up and walked with the mayor to his car, climbing onto the back seat without being told. He asked her again for her name, but she said nothing, and by the time he had left the driveway she was asleep.

The roads in the upper town were too narrow and muddied to drive through. He parked where the tar road tapered into dirt, locked the doors and put on the alarm. On his shoes the mud had dried and faded, cracking at the place where his toes bent. He stepped carefully onto the dirt road, but his feet sank and the mud began to layer again. He glanced behind him to where the girl was standing at the car, looking at the burnt town. He called to her and told her to tread carefully, but her feet were already deep in the mud. They walked towards the blackened homes. His shoes were growing heavy and he felt like a fool, slipping all over the road. He stopped at the first person they came to, an old man sitting next to a pile of rubble with his dog lying nearby, and asked where Willem was. The dog raised its head off its paws and looked at the mayor and the girl and then lowered its head again. The old man remained sitting on his haunches, sifting through the pile.

'This is my family,' he said, holding up an unidentifiable article. 'Not one of them is alive any more except me. Not one.'

The mayor asked again if he knew where Willem was. The man looked up from the scraps in front of him. His mouth was empty of teeth and his face was dirty. He pointed in the direction of the church. The mayor did not thank him, kept walking. The girl remained, staring at the old man as he continued to examine the rubble. The dog came up to her, wagging its tail and sniffing at her hands. It could smell the bread on her fingers and began to lick them. After a distance the mayor turned and called to her. She followed him, the dog behind her.

The church was still standing. In later years people would speak of it as a miracle, but the truth was that the area around the church was bare of plants, worn down by the trampling of parishioners; there had been nothing along which the fire could burn its way to the building. It stood small and blackened from the smoke, the windows splintered and dirty. In the low bell tower a small shrub was blooming from a crack, its flowers grey with ash. They found Willem in the graveyard behind the church. He was young, somewhere past twenty, and strong. Two fresh graves had been dug; he was starting on the third. The earth that he shovelled into heaps was orange in colour, and that colour had caked his shirt and hands and trousers.

'The fire?' the mayor asked, indicating the graves.

'One of them. The other two were old people who couldn't take the cold.'

'You've taken your time about burying them.'

'Too much mud. We had to wait for it to dry a bit.'

The mayor pointed over at the girl, who had strayed to the other end of the graveyard, 'Anyone missing someone?'

'No.'

'But someone?'

'No. Never seen her before. We can ask around but I'm pretty sure she's not from here.'

'Well, she can stay here until I find out more.'

Willem shook his head and gestured at the town. 'Where? We don't even have homes for ourselves.'

'But what am I supposed to do with her?'

'Take her home.'

'What are you saying? Do you think I want all the fucking orphans of the world coming to my doorstep? I am already taking money out of my own pocket to help after this fire!'

Willem did not look at him. His mouth opened and it seemed as though he might say something. Instead, he breathed out heavily and, raising the shovel, returned to digging up the orange dirt. The mayor stood and waited. When it became clear that nothing else would follow, he walked away, shouting at the girl to keep up. There was little else he could do.

After breakfast she washed the dishes and dried them. She waited for her husband to leave before she got dressed and then she left the house, walking down towards the beach. In the road, near the drains, were puddles of yellow mud in which the footprints of small birds could be seen. She stepped around them, careful not to disturb the patterns. Most days, carrying a watering can, wearing a dress with pockets, she went to the beach. Years before her husband had warned her not to walk any sort of distance on the shore, advising her to stay close to the town.

'You can't trust them,' he had said. 'I know them. They will rape and murder you without blinking an eye.'

But with time, seeing that his threats would not keep her away from the beach, hearing her excuses about fresh air and collecting shells, he had hired labourers from the upper town to haul boulders and rocks into place, forming a semi-circle of water, cut off from the sea, large enough to swim in. The area had its own beach, which was seamed in at both sides, and when the tide was low there were rock pools. The inhabitants, even before its completion, called it the Mayor's Wife's Beach. A name that taunted her, and yet, her own name had ceased to have any meaning for her. The sound and shape of it, the absurd backward echo of its two syllables: An-na, An-na, an-na-an-na-an-na. It was a child's babbling, a song of mockery. Made more so by her husband's words, 'I had this done for you, Anna. It is best not to stray from this area, okay?'

However, in its way the beach was a haven. Their house, the first one to which she had been brought, knowing nothing of the town, the people, was small. He had not been the mayor then and it was all he had been able to afford. A single bedroom, lounge and kitchen, with empty double-storey houses on three sides, so that the sea was an absence only. He had pointed at the view from the kitchen window, showing a dry riverbed, tops of houses beyond it: 'You must stay away from those people. If they come near you, you scream or run.'

'Why?' she had asked.

'It's just safer that way. Do you understand? They are dangerous. Just stay away from them.'

With these instructions Anna had little with which to fill the long hours of her husband's working days. From morning to late at night he would be gone, coming home in the dark, a stranger. At times she watched the gardeners and domestic workers make their way down the slope in the early morning into the lower town, waiting for their return in the evening, backs bent against the hill. She watched, too, the sky, the changing shadows on the plains, and in the distance, raised metres above the land, a railway line. Here six times a day, less by night, freight trains transported iron ore from a mine in the north to Saldanha on the coast. The monotony of their passage was dreadful; more than two hundred freighters moving with continuous rhythm, a sound peculiar to them alone. In the night that sound would wake her, so that long after they had passed, echoes of them remained in her husband's breathing.

He bought other houses in quick succession, becoming confused during his absences about where he lived, ordering additions that they did not need and which he forgot about – a half-enclosed porch, four bathrooms, a guest bedroom with no windows, and now, too, a second storey that they would never use. The builders tore down walls, smashed windows. They tramped through the house crushing cement and plant matter into the carpets. They sat where they liked, yelled. To Anna, each room, whether new or old, became frightening in its excess and noise.

'Let them go. We have enough now,' she begged Pieter.

'Don't you want a house that we can be proud of? I want the kind of home neither of us ever had.'

'There's so much noise… and so many rooms. We don't need so many.'

'We'll use them, don't worry. I have plans for all of them.'

'The dirt…' she began.

In her pausing, he looked over to where she sat, aware suddenly of how pale she had become. Dust had settled on her hair, her eyebrows, flakes lay in the poolings of her collar bones. He fancied that were she to get up her silhouette would remain on the chair, marked out in dust.

'How long have you been sitting here?' he asked.

She shrugged, dust lifting at the movement.

People were hired. Maria Geduld as cleaning woman, her husband, Charles, as gardener. Very clearly the mayor explained their jobs to them: keep things clean and organised on the property. He was relying on them to take care of everything; his wife was unwell. He did not want her troubled.

In this way the empty spaces of the house became filled, and those few places which had for a time been Anna's, now changed possession. She remained only in the sound of a floorboard creaking, or the wet in a basin after washing her hands. The small of her back left brief depressions in the pillows of armchairs, before making way for the other woman to work.

Respite came with the weeks of rain and the fire. Construction could not continue in the wet. The dust vanished with the builders. Maria and Charles, homeless after the fire, were given time off to resettle. But the house was too large in its silence. With the return of the sun Anna went down to the beach as before.

'Here she comes,' they would say, those four or five of the aged who sat on the porch of the store day in and day out. 'Coming for her fresh air and shells.'

In houses along the street, maids looked up, watching her slow walk, clicking their tongues. Later they would talk about her: 'I thought she's supposed to be sick.'

'No, no! Trust me, there's nothing wrong with her! Just lazy and rich!'

'That's it. She thinks she's better than us, living with the whites down in the lower town, as though she is a queen or something.'

'Well, all I can say is that I'd be ashamed, living like that, while my own people work themselves to death for me.'

'We're not her people; she's not even from here.'

'That's worse then. Anyway, we're more her people than they are.'

Few others went to the Mayor's Wife's Beach. It was covered with broken shells, sharp underfoot. Anna wore shoes always, stepping carefully. She looked among the rocks; orange stones with round pockets carved into them by the waves. In these lived snails, mussels, small creatures she did not know the names of. There was a rectangle of cement where the beach met the pavement on which a concrete bench was placed. It had been ordered by the mayor and bore a plaque with her name and the date of its placement. Around it she kept a garden of potted plants, unyielding in the heavy salt wind. After watering them, she sat on the bench and looked out at the small beach with its semicircle of rocks.

If she angled her neck correctly she could see part of the cliffs where the shacks of the upper town were spreading. Just behind and below, she knew, lay the small bay where the fishing boats were kept. Most of the boats were rotten and useless, their owners having given up, but in the water she could see two boats, small against the cliffs and the sea. She knew that after the fire many had made homes for themselves in the abandoned rooms of the fish factory and she could hear them now, calling to each other. She was not able to see them and she could not make out what they were saying, there was only the slow carrying of voices on the breeze. She craned her head, her body rising from the bench. She remembered, then, the people watching her from the shop and turned her head back to the semicircle of rocks, the sun overhead, the sea grey and still.

After the fire, at the mayor's request, the ladies of the town had come together and organised a daily meal of soup and bread for those from the upper town, financed by a small government fund. Anna had asked to join them and they had welcomed her, yet when she arrived on the first day they had smiled at her and told her not to trouble herself. For a while she had tried to help, picking up empty dishes, carrying tureens, but they had insisted she do nothing and she had been placed on a chair against the wall to watch as the other women ladled up soup and handed out bread.

The town hall was newly built, bearing commemorative inscriptions both inside and outside with the mayor's name. No mud or dirt was to enter the hall, and in order to prevent such damage they had set up the trestle tables outside. From eleven o'clock the queue started forming. Men from the lower town took it in turns to patrol the queue while others stood on their porches or on the pavement, their arms crossed. Their wives chattered, feeling safe, kind. The hungry stood in groups blowing on soup and chewing bread. Some turned and walked back up the steep hill with brimming mugs, taking what they had to share with the sick and the old.

From her bench Anna could hear the hum of the queue forming. She patted her pockets for the token shells and checked the plants one last time. As she passed the porch of the shop, she paused for their queries.

'Did you get many, Mrs Fortuin?'

'No, not many.'

'Never mind. Perhaps the sea will bring more tonight.'

'Perhaps.'

'And the plants?'

'Oh, they grow at their own pace.'

When she was out of earshot they began to murmur.

'A strange one that.'

'So strange.'

'So quiet.'

'She never says anything.'

'Yes, so shy.'

'And young too.'

'Yes, so young still.'

'Where's the boy? I never see him anymore.'

'Started high school, didn't he? That boarding school in Cape Town.'

'That's the trouble. She misses him. A mother needs her child with her.'

'That's true.'

Anna entered the kitchen and he was there, sitting at the table, his head resting between his thumb and forefinger. She had not expected him and was startled. She moved backwards through the door, her feet already on the steps outside when he lifted his head. She did not notice the girl at the table.

'Where have you been?' the mayor asked.

She made no reply, pointing only outwards.

He got up, lifting his jacket from the back of the chair and said, 'This is the girl. She will be staying here until we find her a place. Put her in the outside room. Find out if she has a name. I can't make any headway with her.'

When he spoke Anna bent her head back, and when he left the room through the further door she shrank back a little, as though he might brush past her in all that distance. After he had left she entered the room again. She stood beside the table and the girl watched her from the corner of her eye. Anna looked like a stranger to the room, as though she had never been in it before. A smell of fried eggs and milk came from the countertop. She moved from where she stood and filled the kettle, made tea. They sipped it, Anna holding her mug in both hands. At the sink water was dripping from the cold tap. Eventually the girl spoke, 'My name is Sara.'

And Anna looked up, surprised by her voice.

She took the girl to the outside room. It was separate from the house, a remainder from the previous owner. There were spider webs in the corner, and the curtains, when she opened them, released dust into the air. She felt annoyed with Maria for not having cleaned there, and then felt shamed by her annoyance. She held in her arms clean bedding and an old dress. The girl carried socks and shoes. After they put the covers on the bed they stood looking at it a while, rubbing the duvet smooth with their open hands.

'You're not from here?' Anna asked.

The girl shook her head.

'Me neither. I had never even seen the sea until the day after I was married.'

She showed the girl into the small bathroom and ran the bathwater for her, pointing out the soap and shampoo, placing a towel on the lid of the toilet seat. She went back into the bedroom and sat on the bed. The girl climbed into the bath and watched the yellow mud from her feet cloud out in the water. Anna was uncertain about what to say. 'Where are you from?' she eventually asked.

'Nowhere now.'

'And before?'

'I don't remember.'

The girl washed her hair, cleaned her nails. She rubbed between each of her toes and she watched the steam settling on the mirror, on the tiles, on the rim of the bath.

'But would you go back?'

'No.'

In the night Sara woke to hear the wind coming in off the sea. The doors and windows rattled and curtains were sucked in and out. The crashing of the waves on the shore was loud and she could not sleep. On the cliffs the shacks leaned back in the wind. Roofs began to shudder. One shack, built too close to the edge, creaked and parted, its walls unclasping before dropping away down the cliff face. Those inside had managed to push past their falling home and stood in alarm in the dark, the sky wide and black overhead, their faces cold in the wind. In the days that followed, the individual parts of that home, the aluminium siding, the planks of wood, the tarpaulin, could be seen moving down the cliff, getting snagged on rock-edges and in bushes, until settling in the gorge below. A gorge no person could descend, above a beach, four metres wide and pebbled, which no person had ever touched.

They ate breakfast together. The three of them in silence, scraping their knives and forks. Sara sat in the same chair as the day before. By now she knew the pattern of scars on the table. After the meal the mayor thanked his wife and left for his office, a small building, white, next to the town hall. He did not kiss his wife goodbye and she did not raise her head to acknowledge his departure. At the door, turning, he looked to where she sat as though he expected a late response, but there was none.

Anna cleared the table and began washing the dishes. Suds wetted the rolled-up sleeves of her cardigan. The girl remained seated at the table.

'I am going to the beach,' Anna said.

The girl nodded.

'You could come? There's not much else to do.'

The girl kept her eyes on the table and listened as the woman rinsed a plate. The porcelain clinked against the sink and the girl thought to herself that it was a long time since she had heard that sound.

'I would rather stay here if I can. Maybe tomorrow.'

Anna put the last plate on the drying rack and passed the cloth over the sink.

'That's fine. We all want to be alone sometimes.'

Later, after Anna had left, Sara stayed in the kitchen. She enjoyed the size of the room; four walls, a high ceiling, windows and two doors. The windows were closed and no air entered the room. She felt warm and contained on all sides. From the chair she counted up the number of cupboards, drawers. She tried to measure the width and height of the room by sight. On the floor under the table were the scratch marks of chairs having been moved in and out. Under her chair, she noticed, there were fewer markings. When she was sure that enough time had passed, she approached the fridge. She found a slab of cheese and bit off a chunk, she ate four tomatoes whole and drank soda from the bottle. In a cupboard she found biltong and in another she found a small fruitcake. It had been some time since she had been able to eat as much as she wanted. The taste of food, of all different types of food, made her mouth ache. She filled it up, kept filling, chewing and swallowing fiercely. On a shelf above the kettle she came across a tin of hot chocolate powder. She grabbed a fistful of the powder and put it in her mouth. It puffed out into her throat, making her cough, before softening on her tongue. When she looked up Willem was standing at the back door. One of his hands was on the handle and in the other he was holding a hat. Brown spittle traced the shape of her mouth, spreading as she tried to swallow. He noticed a smudge on her neck, her hand still in the tin. He remembered the girl then as he had seen her the day before, standing among the graves. He had never seen her before that and she had meant nothing to him, surrounded by the dead. Her body had been an outline, her face invisible. Now she stood before him, with her open mouth, and he could not blink. The room had fallen away around him and he could see only that there were about twelve steps between them. He gripped his hat and took one step forward.

'I'm looking for the mayor.'

The rain came again in the late morning. In the week of sun the windowpanes had met with salt and sand carried on the breeze. The rough shapes of past raindrops were sketched on the panes, clouding the glass. Earlier the mayor had hunched at the window, peering through the stains and through the gap between the two houses behind his office. He could see the bench where his wife sat, the blur of shoulders and hair. She had been motionless, remaining so for a long time. His back had started to ache. Once the rain began, he had drawn the blinds. He did not want to know if she stayed.

Now he was making phone calls. For four days he had been phoning various government branches and organisations, explaining the damage done by the recent fire, the need for provisions, housing. Each time his call had been redirected. Eventually he had been advised about forms to complete. He had stayed up all night filling them in, returning them by fax before sunrise. On this morning he began by phoning the many who had not returned his calls. They were out to tea, in a meeting. Those he did speak to said much the same: 'Yes, yes, we understand. We understand, but there is no money. We are already giving you as much as we can.'

He reminded them about the papers he had faxed, only to be informed, 'Yes, we have them, but there is no money.'

He asked if there were other forms. 'Yes,' he was told, 'but there is still no money.' His situation was not unique, they explained. The people would have to make do with what they could.

'It's an emergency,' he said. 'We are going to run out of food.'

'When you run out of food,' they said, 'we will send a helicopter with supplies. More than that we cannot give you.'

Before noon he received a phone call from his publisher. For two years, together with Dr Terence Pearson, a retired historian living on the slopes of the lower town, the mayor had researched and written *New Monomotapa: The History of the Soutbek Region*. Relating the surprising history of the founding of the town, it had been launched the previous night as a landmark study in terms of its contradiction of the established view of colonial history in South Africa. It proved the existence of a utopian idyll right there on the West Coast some 350 years ago. A society where coloniser and colonised lived together as equals during a period in which conflict and destruction were thought to have dominated the Dark Continent. He had been unable to attend, as had the professor. The roads were still flooded. There was no way out of the town. But his publisher assured him that in spite of their absence the launch had been a success. A number of journalists had expressed interest in interviewing the authors. A television news crew wanted to do a documentary about Soutbek. Several magazines were preparing to run articles with photo spreads of the area. Remembering the burnt houses, the dirt and the chaos, the mayor felt only dismay. It was impossible with the roads closed and the return of the rain, impossible, impossible to hope to repair anything in time.

The phone on his desk rang again. It was a reporter from the *Daily Sentinel*, asking him about the book, what it revealed about South African history. He read his responses from notes the professor had made for him concerning misconceptions about the impossibility of peaceful co-existence, not only between black and white, but between people of indigenous tribes as well.

'Soutbek is the *omphalos*,' he said, stumbling over the word, 'the birth place of assimilation and integration.'

'But why does it matter now?' the reporter asked. 'Apartheid ended almost two decades ago. Do people really care about that sort of thing anymore?'

The mayor faltered. 'No,' he said. 'No, you do not understand the significance of this history. South Africa is not only about Apartheid; it is not only about black and white. Remember we are the Rainbow Nation, a nation made up of the blood of Malay slaves, of Dutch, French, English, of the Khoi and the San and all the tribes of South Africa, and many nationalities beyond our own borders. Do you see,' he continued, 'that is what Soutbek represents. It represents the entire past of South Africa. South Africa as we know it, as a rainbow society, was not born at Cape Town as so many believe, it was born here.'

The interviewer thanked the mayor. 'I will send a photographer for a follow-up piece once the roads are okay.'

'Listen,' the mayor said, 'listen, you might not think this is important, but it is.'

'Of course it is,' the interviewer replied before hanging up.

The mayor looked at the notes in front of him, trying to remember the answers he had given.

He was sitting in the half-dark when Willem entered.

'I see you haven't found the girl's family.'

He reached for the light switch. The room smelled cold, of cement and paint. There were no pictures on the walls and the carpet was too small so that flecks of paint could be seen where wall and floor met. The desk, large and mahogany, was in the centre, bearing a green and gold lamp, a desk calendar and a telephone. There was an armchair in front of the desk, but Willem did not sit in it. The office was new, built along with the town hall, separated from it by a narrow path and a line of daisy bushes. They could hear the chatter from the food queue, the voice of a man shouting, 'Keep in line, keep in line!'

The mayor sighed. He had forgotten about the girl. Gesturing in the direction of his house he said, 'She won't talk. I need to phone social services, I just haven't had a chance. And now this rain again.'

He looked at the closed blinds and then down at his desk. After a minute he remembered Willem. 'Was there something you wanted?'

Willem told him about the shack that had fallen from the cliff the night before.

'For God's sake, can't something be done about that mess?' He was standing now, fiddling with the cords of the blinds.

'You're the mayor,' Willem said.

'What do you expect me to do? This is a rural community. We have no money. I gave out blankets, we're supplying them with food. This rain. No one can get here. The roads are closed. We're going to run out of food. I've made phone calls. The government says we already get a food subsidy, they have no more money for us. But how does a subsidy help us if we can't get to food to buy with it? They say they'll helicopter food in if it continues, but only if it is an emergency. What is more of an emergency than this?'

'And the new hall?'

'What about it?'

'Couldn't people be housed there temporarily?'

'It's brand new, for God's sake!'

'People are sleeping on the beach without roofs or walls and now the rain is back. They need cover.'

'Let's just wait until this afternoon. Maybe the rain will stop.'

Willem did not reply. They looked at each other.

'And afterwards?' Willem asked.

'Afterwards?'

'When the rain stops. When they can get to us. What then? There are no jobs. There's no money. Since the factory closed…'

'Listen, I do what I can. You know that. We employ as many as we can.'

Willem shook his head. 'The municipality employs six men. What about the rest?'

'Things will change. People are already phoning about the book.'

'And you think a book will change the fact that we have nothing?'

'You'll see,' the mayor replied, impatient now. 'People will come. Our town will be famous and people will come from all over just to see it.'

'Because of a book?' Willem laughed. 'How can a book do that?'

The mayor reached into his drawer, which held several copies of *The History*. 'Here,' he said, holding one out to Willem. 'Read it. You will see.'

Willem remained standing with his hands at his sides.

'Take it, take it,' the mayor urged. 'It's free.'

He reached forward and took the book, and from behind him there was a knock at the door. A man, small and thin, in a grey tracksuit, entered the room.

'Ah, Terence, nice to see you. I have just been on the phone with Hilda about the launch. Willem, you know the professor?'

Willem nodded his greeting. The professor nodded back.

'The professor and I have some things to discuss.'

Willem nodded again at both men. 'I'll be back at three if the rain hasn't stopped.'

'Certainly.'

When it became common knowledge that the professor and the mayor were locked away for hours at a time in the mayor's office, the light burning well into the night, a great mystery presented itself to the town, for though he had never said anything outright, it was widely known that the professor had not been pleased when Pieter Fortuin, a coloured man, was elected mayor of Soutbek. Thinking they could get the answers to the mystery from the mayor's wife, the inhabitants went in twos and threes to visit her. Anna, who had never had visitors before, was overwhelmed by the sudden rush of goodwill.

'Oh, we thought we'd come visit you, since you spend so much time all alone. We've noticed that your husband is so busy lately.'

'Such a busy man. Always working, working.'

'Yes,' Anna replied. 'He takes his job seriously.'

'Of course, yes, we can see. That's why we keep re-electing him, of course.'

Silence filled the room. Everyone waited, sipping their tea, looking at her expectantly. Someone asked, 'When is your son coming?'

'I'm not sure. They have their holidays.'

'What is his name again?'

Anna paused. 'David. His name is David.'

She looked at the lounge in which she had never sat, nor received guests. She knew what was coming and she hated these women with their pencilled-on eyebrows and permed hair.

'You must look forward to seeing him, since your husband has been so busy lately.'

She did not reply.

'What is it that he is doing? Your husband? We see him and the professor together all the time.'

'I can't tell you that,' Anna said, 'I don't know.'

It was not a lie.

Twice a week the professor walked down the hill to the store with a shopping list that had remained unaltered for fifteen years or more. As he passed their houses, the inhabitants of the lower town stopped in their gardens or stood still at their windows to watch him. They looked specifically at his toenails, yellow horns sticking out of his leather sandals; his bare ankles, visible below the seam of his tracksuit, white with scales of dry skin. There were liver spots on his hands, wrinkles on his brow, his hands, his neck and earlobes. His neighbours gossiped that he rarely threw out his rubbish or did laundry. Those who happened to come near him spoke of his old-man smell; the smell of ageing armpits, of secret hollows and folds in the skin. Yet they found it reassuring, this litany of attributes of the genius, as it confirmed that what he carried in his head mattered more to him than the habits of cleanliness which they themselves lived by.

Rumours began to spread that the mystery work of the mayor and professor was a book. No one could think what it might be about. The professor, they'd heard, was an expert in South African pre-colonial tribal history and the mayor, as far as they knew, had never studied or shown any interest in studying. Guesses were made, but there could be no certainty. They watched more closely as the professor walked down the hill. They sidled up to him in the store, as though the secret could be sniffed on him, or simply discovered through the sight of him. He did not return their greetings, ignoring their queries after his health and general activities. They admired him all the more for it.

Having left the mayor's office, Willem stood outside the town hall and looked at the incline of the hill, the steep road. It was still raining. Above him the sky was grey and behind him the sea was grey and green. The black of the street was steaming and he was beginning to feel the wet through his clothes. The image of the girl's face could not be removed from his mind. There was no excuse he could think of for seeing her again. He turned his eyes towards the beach, to where the form of the mayor's wife remained unchanging on her bench. He looked again back up the hill. He walked a little way until he reached a tree, and then, patting the wet pavement, sat down to wait. The book the mayor had given him was heavy on his lap. Willem sheltered it with his hands, careful to protect the cover as far as he could from the rain.

Rumours of Gold

For the first two years after Jan van Riebeeck's arrival in 1652 as Commander of the Cape refreshment station, nothing was known of the interior further than 100 miles. Concerned more with profit than with geographical exploration, the Verenigde Oost-Indische Compagnie (voc) did not encourage journeys into the hinterland. Van Riebeeck and his men focused their attention on building a fort and growing produce to feed the passing sailors. However, cultivation of crops was difficult, and the local indigenous inhabitants would only trade their diseased and old livestock. Van Riebeeck grew frustrated with what he described as *'een arm ende ellendich leven'* (a poor and pitiful life). As his frustration mounted, he began to look for new ways of making the refreshment station a success, in order to speed his promotion and removal from the Cape. He had heard, through travelogues, rumours and idle gossip, of the fabled land of Monomotapa which was believed to be situated somewhere to the far north of the Cape. Monomotapa supposedly boasted the river Spiritu Sancto, upon the banks of which numerous wealthy cities were located, among others, the legendary Vigiti Magna. It was from these cities that the Portuguese were rumoured to acquire much gold. Van Riebeeck requested permission from the Heeren xvii, directors of the voc, to send a small party into the interior in order to ascertain whether arable land could be found, trade with the indigenous people could be established, and most importantly, whether the fabled Monomotapa could be reached. Permission was granted and van Riebeeck went about assembling a party of volunteers for *'een tocht na Monomotapa'* (an expedition to Monomotapa). There was no shortage of willing bodies, for in those days the voc held the promise of adventure, and many young men joined as private soldiers in order to lay claim to some of that adventure. Van Riebeeck drew a map for the men, in which he indicated that the city where the emperor of Monomotapa kept his treasure was

828 miles northeast and 322 miles west of the Cape. The map was based on information gained from accounts by Martinus Martinio, a Spanish priest who was also a celebrated traveller and cartographer. Unfortunately for van Riebeeck, the closest Martinio had been to Africa was when he passed the Cape by sea in 1653 on a voyage to India, without even setting foot on shore. As a result, van Riebeeck's map consisted of various cities and rivers which did not exist.

Prior to the commencement of the expedition, van Riebeeck had learnt from a local woman called Eva about a wealthy and civilised people called the Namaquas, who lived in the North. Eva, a *'Caapse Hottentoo'* (Cape Hottentot), who had dwelled at the fort since she was a child and had been converted to Christianity and then baptised Eva, was used by members of the Compagnie as a translator in their dealings with local tribes. According to Eva, the Namaquas bartered with elephant tusks and had *'bestiael in groote meenichte'* (livestock in great quantities). She also said that they were adorned with much gold and copper jewellery, which led van Riebeeck to believe that they had contact with the inhabitants of Monomotapa. Consequently, he instructed the expedition party to search first for the Namaquas in order to win them over with gifts. They were then to persuade them to bring their livestock to the fort for trade. Furthermore, the explorers were to find out from the Namaquas about the location of Monomotapa, and request a guide or guides from amongst them to lead the way.

Having been given their instructions, and with the promise of double pay for any travelling done further than what their provisions allowed, the party set out. This was the first of six expeditions made during the period of 1660 to 1664 in order to attempt to persuade the Namaqua into trade and to locate the mythical Monomotapa.

The first expedition left the Cape on 12 November 1660 and did not return until 20 January the following year. The party consisted of twelve soldiers and two translators, under the leadership of Jan Danckaert. Unfortunately, Danckaert proved to be an inept leader. He had been chosen owing to his experience in travelling through Italy, but this did not assist him in the sparse terrain of the western interior of South Africa. Very little is remarkable about this journey, other than the fact that the party came upon a river where they sighted up to 300 elephants, naming it therefore *Oliphants reviere* (Oliphants River). They believed this river to be the Spiritu Sancto. After numerous days of travel, the explorers espied *'de vuyren van de Namaquas'* (the fires of the Namaqua), but due to lack of food they were unable to travel further and were compelled to return home. Van Riebeeck viewed the expedition as an utter failure, blaming the men for insubordination and Danckaert for poor leadership: *'de reyse weder genoechsaem vruchteloos... uytgevaleen'* (the journey turned out to be fruitless).

However, the failure did not prevent van Riebeeck from immediately gathering a new team. Ten days after the return of the first company, the second left. Under the leadership of Corporal Pieter Cruijthoff, their mission was to establish facts and find out more about the Namaqua. This they did, recording that the Namaqua were 700 strong, with up to 7,000 livestock. The travellers feasted with them and asked the king, Akembie, to come to the fort for trading purposes. As a parting gift the men were given a goat, an animal which they had not yet seen at the Cape. They returned on 11 March 1661, and van Riebeeck greatly rewarded them for their success.

Again, ten days later a third team was sent out. This time the leader was Pieter van Meerhoff, a junior surgeon, who had been on the previous two expeditions. The party was unable to locate the Namaqua, but they did encounter a group of Grigriqua who had many copper ornaments. After enquiring about these ornaments, van Meerhoff was informed that they came from a town a month's journey away. This was a lie on the part of the Grigriqua, but van Meerhoff was fooled, and it confirmed in his mind the presence of the mythical Vigiti Magna.

As time passed, there was no sign of the Namaqua coming to the fort to trade. Not wanting to travel during the winter, as rains would swell the rivers and make them impassable, van Riebeeck sent the next expedition into the interior on 14 November 1661. They returned three months later on 13 February 1662. The importance placed on this particular journey is clear from the choice of group leader, namely Pieter Everaert, the head of the militia at the Cape. Again, the party encountered the Grigriqua and was told that the Namaqua were far in the interior and could not be reached in the dry season due to lack of water. Noticing that the Oliphants River ebbed and flowed, Everaert followed it to its mouth and reported (incorrectly) that it flowed into an inland sea, rather than the Atlantic Ocean.

In 1662, van Riebeeck's long-wished-for relief from his position as Commander of the Cape occurred and he was succeeded by Zacharias Wagenaar. The Heeren XVII instructed Wagenaar: '*Namaquas wederom op te soecken ende voorts de groote revier Vigiti Magna ende omliggende vaste plaatsen aan te doen*' (to seek the Namaqua again and to explore further the great river Vigiti Magna and surrounding areas). Following in the footsteps of the previous commander, Wagenaar chose Pieter Cruijthoff as group leader. The fifth expedition into the interior commenced on 21 October 1662 and ended on 1 February 1663. This was the first expedition to take a wagon, and they found this mode of travel difficult in the rough terrain. When the explorers met the Namaqua they were informed that they were at war with the Grigiqua, and demanded assistance from the Dutch. The party declined to get involved in the war and was consequently denied further northerly passage by the Namaqua. They tried, by means of subterfuge, to trick the Namaqua but they were caught out and attacked. Injured and ill, they returned home.

The last of the six expeditions was sent out nearly a year after the previous one. The men were given strict instructions to fight the Namaqua if need be, for it now became crucial to find the mythical city. They were also told to bring back as much livestock as possible for the '*Indische retourschepen aenstaande jaer*' (the ships returning from India the following year). On their journey they saw '*twee camelen*' (two camels: these are probably giraffes): '*waer door wij presumeerden dat wij niet verre van de Revier Vigiti Magna waren, wandt ick had voordesen wel hooren seggen van de Namacquas als dat daer omtrent de revier sulcke beesten zich onthiel*' (whereby we presumed that we were not far from the river Vigiti Magna because I had previously heard from the Namaqua that there are such beasts in the vicinity of the river). However, their wagon was burned, their supplies stolen, and they were desperately parched. They had no choice but to return to the fort. The trip was considered a vast let-down.

This final failure ended northern exploration for a time and one official commented that '*De lant rijse naer de groote Rivier Vigiti Magna ende groote stadt Monomotapa ende verwachten negotien in gout en tanden vandaer m[e]ijne maer Chimerique Concepten zyn*' (The land journeys to the great river Vigiti Magna and the great city of Monomotapa, and the expected trade in gold and ivory from there, is a chimera in my view). It would be eighteen years before a trip to the interior was made again, and in the meantime, as the improvement of the fort and cultivation of crops at the refreshment station continued, the Namaqua and Monomotapa were forgotten.

West of the manufactured beach stretched a long shoreline. It continued, partly straight, towards a cliff before turning round a bend and progressing on, out of sight. Anna was not certain about the bend. Perhaps it did end there after all, at that cliff and its mist. Yet she imagined the bend and the bends to follow further along the coastline. She imagined, too, the land coming in flat from the distant mountains, where there lived different plants, people, animals. Her own home had been further inland. There had been mountains at the end of every view, and she found, now, this vast openness on all sides always unexpected.

They had lived on a farm, her father working as a labourer, her mother helping in the kitchen of the main house. Their home was small, a square of cement-brick with a flat roof of aluminium sheets. Inside there was a kitchen in which they ate and sat, and another room in which they slept. In the long nights of the summer months when the heat was unbearable, the children would take the mattresses up onto the roof to sleep. Two to a mattress, watching the stars above them, hearing the barking of bat-eared foxes, they fell asleep with their arms and legs spread out, careful not to touch each other in the heat. They woke to the dawn and the bleating of sheep in the fields, seeing little of their parents, who worked long hours. But on Saturday nights the children gathered around their mother, watching for the staggering form of their father. She had taught them long ago to climb into the thorn trees or onto the roof when they saw him coming like this. Still, from time to time one of them was caught. At church on Sunday mornings they sat in the back pews among other wives and children bearing bruises and welts, their faces drawn, their heads down.

Once, out walking through fields and grazing sheep, Anna came upon a fence of barbed wire. Small wisps of sheep's wool clung to the barbs. She had looked along the length of the fence, seeing that it extended on and on in both directions. Ahead of her, past the field on the other side of the fence, she had seen another fence, and beyond that another. Looking around to the land within view, she had seen that it was all fenced in. Rows and rows of fences cut across the landscape. She had realised then that the land was all taken, that it was all owned and delineated into sections, and that she had no part of it. She had turned, and walked back to the small house on the outskirts of the farm.

Pieter she had always known, as a baby, as a child and on. He was a friend of her father's, and every few months he had come to visit, rousing the dust as he turned his car onto the dirt roads of the farm they lived on. The family had never known anyone who wasn't white to own a car, and they admired him and feared him a little. At the first sign of his approach, the smaller children climbed onto the roof in order to follow the progression of the cloud of dust, while others ran out to meet it. They clamoured around, some afraid to touch it, others stroking the dust from the bonnet and doors.

At that time Pieter earned money by travelling across the country for months on end, selling goods. He had a system of arrangements with warehouse men, who, for a neat price, filled his car with as much merchandise as it could take. Loaded like that, he trekked from rural town to rural town, exchanging, selling, until his car was empty and his pockets were full. By the time he arrived at the farm he would be exhausted. He slept for long portions of each day of his visit. In the afternoons he took the children for a short drive or let them sit in his car, guiding their mimicked steering.

She sought out his company when she could, and with time she found herself disquieted by his departures, restless in anticipation of his arrivals. In the months of his absence she became more and more sombre. With each of his visits it grew increasingly difficult to be near him. Her palms felt hollow, her head hurt.

They had walked out into the fields together. He had touched her arm.

'Where did you get these bruises?' he asked.

Anna looked at the blue marks next to his fingers. It was clear that they had been made by a gripping hand. She glanced up. 'Please...'

'You know,' he said, walking on, 'we have a lot in common. I also had an unhappy childhood.'

He told her about the town he came from beside the sea, how his father had been a fisherman in Soutbek for decades; that he had grown up knowing the smell of fish and seawater. His father had gone out fishing one morning and two days later his body had washed up on the rocks, his throat cut. There had been no official investigation into the death. That year the fish factory had raised their quota per individual fisherman and the new system had caused fighting. Fish were not as plentiful as before. Longer hours were needed on the water in order to get a decent catch. If they did not meet the quota they would not be paid, their children would not be fed. At times men had fought each other over a single fish. He told Anna that since the day he saw his father's body on the rocks beside the factory, he had known that he would never be a fisherman. He told her that he was working hard to keep it that way.

'I'll never be caught out like that,' he said. 'I'll be the one cutting throats. I will not be poor. I will not work myself to death so that my family starves while some rich man gets richer!'

Anna looked at the ground.

'I have great plans,' he continued, 'but I am biding my time. Don't they say that everything comes to those who wait?'

'Maybe. I don't know.'

'They do. That's exactly what they say.'

She began walking in a different direction. He followed her, and for a time there was silence. Again he tried to take hold of her arm, but she drew away.

'Wait a minute. Don't move,' he said, turning towards a bush, lifting a tortoise which had been resting there.

'Don't!' she called.

'Wait there, I said.'

He bent down again and picked an orange flower that was growing nearby. Facing her, he put the tortoise on the ground, placed the flower on the tortoise's back. For a minute it stayed still, its limbs evenly tucked in, but soon it began to walk towards her where the unsteady rhythm of its movements rocked the shell against her feet. Anna laughed then, with her head back. He came forward and kissed her, her hair whipping against his ear.

When Pieter left the next morning she had been too shy to speak to him and in the intervening months she walked around, crushed by her own timidity.

It was at dusk several months later that the children noticed the cloud of dust approaching. She ran into the house and tried to smooth her hair in front of the mirror. In it she saw her face, small, her cracked lips, the sharp bones of her chest and shoulders. She looked at the room behind her. It was filled with mattresses, worn clothes, blankets. On the wall next to the mirror was a collection of framed photographs of the dead, their faces just visible after years of exposure to the sun. The photographs did not belong to her family; they had been there when her father and mother had moved into the house, already nailed to the wall, already somewhat bleached. There was nothing to tie Anna to these people, other than a single wall of the house. Yet there was something she understood in their expressions of self-consciousness above their high collars, their starched Sunday bests, and she could not prevent herself from envying them their clean faces, their neatly tied-back hair. The sound of his car neared. There was nothing else in the room; nothing with which she could make herself look better. She glanced at her reflection once more before climbing through the window and hiding behind the house.

Night had fallen by the time she allowed herself to enter again. Pieter was sitting at the kitchen table with her parents and the children. He nodded at her, not interrupting his speech.

'I've stopped travelling,' he was saying. 'After years of work I finally have enough money to put down on a house in what used to be the white part of Soutbek. They can't keep me out any more. Things are changing and I am going to be part of that change.' He paused to make sure that everyone was listening. 'I have great plans,' he said. 'I won't be kept poor and starving. I won't allow myself to be poor.'

His voice had been steadily rising, and he stood up then, motioning with both hands. His gesture took in the small room, the children, the rest of the house, the whole farm. 'You don't have to live like this. There's no reason. Things are changing. Look at me! Look what I have done for myself.'

Her father grunted. Both men were drunk, she could tell. The smaller children, huddled around the mother, stared at Pieter wide-eyed.

'Look at you!' Pieter continued. 'You live like an animal. You work like an animal; your children live like animals! You beat them like they are animals. For what? For what? For no money, for a *dop* once a week? What kind of life is that? How can you be satisfied to live like that?'

There was a crash and her father was on his feet, the chair knocked over. He was roaring, but she could not make out any words. They – her mother, the children, herself – looked on. They made no sound. He moved towards the other man, his face livid, his chest heaving. He was drunk, bellowing. As he moved, his arms reaching out for Pieter, her father's body suddenly collapsed beneath him and he was on the floor. He clutched at the table legs, at the legs of Pieter. He could not raise himself off the ground. Humiliated and drunk, crawling, he made his way to the door, out into the night.

The farmer arrived in the early morning, before dawn, climbing out of his *bakkie* with a shotgun in one hand. In the back sat her father. Above his left temple was a deep gash. His face was black with blood and his shirt was torn. Blood of a brighter colour covered his clothes. His head was down. He did not raise his eyes. From the house his wife and children came forward slowly. The farmer addressed her mother 'This son of a bitch killed one of my sheep last night. Then he tore it apart like a fucking savage and danced around the main house spreading its innards everywhere.'

Anna's mother clutched at the children around her. '*Baas*,' she said, 'I'm sorry, *Baas*. He had a *dop* in.'

'I don't care how much he had to drink! He tried to set my house alight. He shouted obscene things at my wife and children.'

'*Baas*, I'm sorry, *Baas*.'

'He's a savage!'

Her mother wrung her hands in her apron. Anna looked to where her father sat and then back at the farmer. Pieter was standing in the doorway, squinting out at the scene. His top lip was raised, his teeth bared.

The farmer pointed at her father where he sat on the back of the *bakkie*. 'Get down from there. I'm sick of drunken shits like you. You and your family can go to hell. Pack your things and *voetsek*. Do you understand what I am saying, *dronkgat*? I am telling you and your *nikswerd* family to get the fuck off my land and never come back!'

Her mother pulled her apron over her head and began to cry. They had no place to go. Her father sat on a rock in front of the house and would speak to nobody. Pieter came outside, climbing into his car where he sat with the doors locked. Two of the boys tried all the handles, pleading to be let in, but he looked straight ahead. Anna went into the house; began putting things into piles, folding clothes into small bundles. She worked steadily at gathering their possessions. Though there was little, she was uncertain how they would carry it all. Later, looking out of the window, she saw Pieter and her father talking together with grim faces. Yet it seemed that they had made peace; they were shaking hands.

Towards afternoon Pieter came to find her. He led her outside. Under the acacia tree he pulled her towards him.

'We are going to be married,' he said. 'I spoke to your father. And we are to be married, if you want. I will give you a home and I will look after you. There will be nothing to trouble you anymore.'

Above her the sun was bright and the white thorns of the acacia tree looked sharp, bone-like. Behind her the crumbling house, the mattresses still on the roof, was silent and small. Around her all was quiet; the deep long fields, the mountains high in the sunlight. She looked at everything, and she said, 'Yes.'

In the late afternoon they stood outside the house. Their backs, even those of the smallest children, were laden with possessions. Her father still wore the torn, bloodied shirt. Her mother's eyes were red from crying and she wiped them on her sleeves. The children looked frightened, very small. Anna felt sick. She had not thought of this. She had not really thought of this happening.

'Can't they...?' she asked, turning to Pieter.

'No,' he said. 'There is no room.'

She began to cry. 'But... can't they just...?'

'No,' he said again. 'No.'

The bare feet of her brothers and sisters were lined up before her. She thought of them walking in the dust, on the roads, through bushes, endlessly, without destination.

'They have nowhere to go,' she said.

'This is what your father chose for himself,' he said. 'I have my own plans. There is no place for them.'

She said her goodbyes and climbed into the car. As they drove away from the small home and the farm, she tried to look back, but the dust on the road behind them was too dense for any view to remain.

'I gave your father money,' he said. 'They won't starve.'

On the bench, Anna became aware of the rain falling on her. In the distance she could see strange fannings of orange where the rain had caused rivulets to wash soil down from the land onto the shore. Gulls rose and fell over the waves. She gathered her watering can and shells and began walking home. In the road near the house she saw Willem, sitting with the book.

'You're wet,' she said.

'So are you.'

She wiped her hand over the front of her dress, as though this movement would dry her.

'Come in for some tea,' she said.

The kitchen was empty, the house silent. He sat at the table while she went to the outside room and looked through the window. The girl was asleep on the bed, her legs curled to her chin, her mouth open. She returned to the kitchen and made the tea, placed biscuits on a plate. They drank in silence. At every sound he turned his head to the door, but she did not appear. After his tea he smiled and thanked her, walking home in the rain, forgetting his conversation with the mayor and the homeless still on the beach.

THE FOUND JOURNAL OF PIETER VAN MEERMAN

The six expeditions which took place between 1660 and 1664 were authorised by the Heeren XVII and were conducted under the official aegis of the Compagnie. Specific guidelines were laid out for each group of explorers, with one person from each group selected as the official journal keeper. It was his job to record the following: compass directions; the period of time taken to traverse between landmarks; areas of arable land or water-courses; animal and plant-life encountered; as much information as possible about the native peoples they came across; whether the native people would be willing to trade and have a friendly relationship with the Dutch; and finally, which tribes were at war with each other and which were allies. On the return of the expedition to the fort these journal entries were copied into the *Dagh Register* so that the information could be made use of in further expeditions.

Up until now it has been believed that the six recorded journeys were the only explorations into the interior throughout this period. However, recently, during reconstruction work done on one of the original stone houses in the Soutbek region of the West Coast, an old handwritten manuscript was discovered, wrapped in goatskin. It transpired that this manuscript was the journal kept by one Pieter van Meerman, the self-appointed leader of an unauthorised expedition in search of Monomotapa in 1662. Made up of a group of eight '*vryburghers*' (free citizens) and one '*Hottentoo tolcq*' (Hottentot translator), the expedition set out in secret, without the permission of the Compagnie. The *Dagh Register* at the Cape makes no mention of the disappearance of seven men, nor is there any acknowledgement of it in unofficial sources. It can only be assumed that the reason behind the disappearance of these men was unknown and unremarkable to their fellow colonisers. The recent unexpected discovery of the van Meerman text has not only shone new light on the early history of South Africa, but has also given new insight into the relationship between the colonisers and indigenous peoples of South Africa in the seventeenth century. As such, it is the record of the unknown expedition which makes up the focus of this book; for these brave explorers, after countless adventures, discovered a treasure far greater than the fabled gold of Monomotapa. The form of this treasure will become apparent as the tale of these explorers unfolds.

The information in this study is pieced together from the records of Pieter van Meerman. Unfortunately he was an undisciplined, sporadic and untidy journal-keeper at the best of times; consequently there are several illegible entries as well as numerous gaps. Furthermore, due to the extreme age of the manuscript, it is understandable that the text is in poor condition. Damage done by damp and rodents over the years has resulted in large lacunae. However, the account which follows here is, to the best of our knowledge, true and correct.

In the early evening Sara awoke. The covers were warm around her, the same warmth on her breath. She could hear the rain on the roof, the waves on the shore below. She was hungry and her limbs, idle, stretched out under the covers. For a while she yawned, and lay as she was. Eventually she rose, dressed herself, washed her face and combed her hair flat against her neck, wetting it first. There was no shelter between her room and the back door, and she had to dash across the yard in the rain.

In the kitchen Anna was rolling dough. A long fat slab was positioned before her. There was flour on the table, the floor, on her face and hands. The sink held used mixing bowls, the sideboard was littered with ingredients. She rolled the dough backwards and forwards, lifting it and slapping it back down before continuing to thin it out in all directions. When she heard the girl, she looked up, pushing hair out of her face with a wrist. 'The eggs are past their expiry dates. I thought I'd use them while I still can.'

Sara could smell the raw dough, the warmth of the oven as it began to heat in the corner. Her stomach growled. She walked to the sink, running her fingers along the bowls, licking them clean. She leaned against the sideboard and watched the woman's shoulders as her arms rolled the dough. When Anna turned to the cupboard, Sara reached forward and tore a strip, small, from the dough. She held it under her tongue and wished for that strip to swell. Anna showed her how to cut out the round shapes of the biscuits. She used a butter knife to trace the rim of a glass placed downwards on the dough, spacing each one carefully, so that there was no waste. They packed six trays, baking them for twenty minutes each. The kitchen was filled with the scent of baking. When the biscuits came out of the oven, the girl sat at the table, watching the steam rise from them, feeling the taste of them on the air. She sat on her hands until Anna said they were cool enough to eat. Then she ate one and put three in her pocket for when she was alone.

It was late when the mayor came home. The girl was already asleep. Anna was in the kitchen, counting biscuits into packets. He took off his wet jacket and shook it. A brown envelope fell onto the floor. She looked at it as he bent to pick it up.

'He was here earlier. I think he was waiting for it,' she said.

'I forgot. I'll take it later.'

'In the rain?'

He ignored her question, pointed at the biscuits, 'What's this?'

'I thought we could distribute them. There aren't many, but we could share them out to some.'

'They need protein, fruit, vegetables. Proper food. Not cake and biscuits.'

'Can't they have biscuits too?'

'They can have biscuits. Let them eat all the fucking biscuits they want! And when their gums start bleeding and the children have rickets then who's to blame? I'll get the blame! And this fucking rain won't mean a fucking thing to anyone because it will all be my fault.'

'The helicopters will come. They said... the rain. It will stop soon.'

He sat down at the table and she brought him his dinner from the warming drawer. He ate, watching her work. After a while she said, 'They don't let me help with the soup, and I just thought...'

'The what?'

'The soup. They don't want me there.'

He grunted and continued forking food into his mouth until he had cleared the plate. He carried it to the sink and poured himself a glass of water. Then he went to the bedroom and put on his rubber boots and rain jacket. When he returned to the kitchen she had placed a plastic bag on the table for him. It held a packet of biscuits, a few tins of food, potatoes, apples and teabags.

'It's all we have at the moment.'

He took the bag from her and went to the door.

'Wait,' she called, running from the room. 'Just a minute.'

Coming back, she handed him a jersey and a pair of socks. He pulled the hood of his jacket over his head and went out into the dark and the rain.

As the mayor approached the upper town, the glow of individual fires became visible. He saw the remains of charred electrical poles that rose between the plots, their wires, limp, hanging. There was nothing to be done about them until the town was reachable again, and even then, there was little hope. Most of the upper town had been without electricity for a few years. The last fire had seen to that. It was little matter anyhow, for those in the upper town did not have money. Whether they had electricity or not they would not have been able to pay for it. They would still have used fire for warmth and cooking.

From the shadows he could make out the forms of dogs. They barked at him, but came no closer. He was surprised by their numbers; thin and wet with rain. In the dwellings that he passed he could hear voices. In some, people could be heard singing, in some there was talking. In others, piles of rubble only, dark and uninhabited now, there was silence. He passed burnt gardens, broken fences of chicken wire. Where there had been flowers there was now muddied ash. He entered Willem's street, his head down in the rain. When he came to the house all was black and wet. The roof and walls were broken, lying on the ground in pieces. The plots on either side were filled with rubble too. Nothing moved in or around that mass. The rain drove into his face and he realised that he did not know where Willem was living now.

Across the road there was a shack, framed out of wooden boards and black bags. He called a greeting, and moved aside the plastic covering the doorway. Inside the small space were children, women and men, an old couple. In the centre of the room, in a shallow metal drum, was a fire. They looked up at him without interest, their faces orange in the firelight. He apologised for interrupting them, asked if they knew where Willem was living. They looked at each other and then one of them spoke, saying he had heard that Willem had moved into the Cupido place.

'Yes,' the mayor said, 'I know where it is.'

He reached into his pocket and brought out his wallet. It held only a few coins and a R100 note. He took out the note and wasn't sure what to do. One of the younger men stepped forward and held out his hand. The mayor placed the note in his hand, thanking them all. They wished him well, and he withdrew, walking on.

The Cupido house was unoccupied, had been so for the years since a previous fire. The wife had been a seamstress, taking in sewing from the lower town when the fish supply ran low. She had worked in her kitchen, cutting patterns on a large pine table, sewing with an old pedal-operated machine. Most days the husband brought home fish for a meal, but not more.

Nobody saw the fire start. It spread without pattern, moving through all places at once. In their house the Cupidos became separated by smoke. She ushered the children through the back door, fearing for their youngest, a toddler still. Him she had not been able to find. About to return to the inner rooms, she saw her husband, already outside, a bundle in his arms. He was leading the children down to the shore. Knowing to rescue that which would put food on the table afterwards, she grabbed the sewing machine. It was heavy, mounted on a metal frame, with wheels that stuck in the sand as she pulled. Some distance away a crowd had formed. Individuals were screaming, crying. They asked each other who had been seen, who hadn't. In the light of the flames their faces vanished and reappeared, an array of frightful masks. Amongst them she marked her husband, his deliberate step towards her, the sob as he recognised what it was that she dragged behind her. In his arms the bundle became clear to her. It was not a child. He had rescued his fishing nets.

After the fire they had found the boy, a small purple thing, unrecognisable. He had suffocated from the smoke, in his sleep, they said. There was no pain, they told the parents. But his eyes were open where he lay and his tongue was thick in his mouth from coughing. The Cupidos did not return to the house. With their remaining children they moved to another town, where the wife had family. The toddler was buried in the cemetery of the upper town, along with others who had died that night. There was no money for a headstone to mark his grave. Instead, his mother collected pebbles from the beach and used them to cover the small mound of earth. With time, rain and wind had smoothed the earth, scattered the stones. Plants grew in that place now, flowering in the spring.

Initially out of respect for the dead, the house had been avoided. But as the months passed and it became clear that the Cupidos would not return, it was ransacked. Nothing was left other than a burnt fridge, which at one point had been carried from the kitchen and then abandoned halfway through the lounge. The house became the night-time haunt of teenagers who went there to smoke and drink, have sex. Children played there during the day, reading out loud the graffiti which had begun to cover the walls.

In April of the following year the Lewendal girl went missing during a game of hide-and-seek. The members of the upper town came together to look for her. They combed the beach, the fish factory, the scrublands behind them. Some time later a group of teenagers, smoking *dagga* in the house, opened the abandoned fridge and found her body, small and stiff inside.

After that the Cupido house was thought to be cursed. While the exact details were altered over time, a legend of sorts grew up around it. Children were warned not to go there. People averted their eyes when they walked past. It became a house both remembered and forgotten.

There had been no other place for Willem to take his mother and sister after the recent fire. He knew the Cupido house; knew it still had much of its roof; that no other family would claim it. Trudie cried at her brother's suggestion. 'There has to be somewhere else. We can't live there. There has to be somewhere else.'

'There isn't. Ma is sick. She can't stay on the beach.'

Nor could she stay among others in the large rooms of the abandoned factory. The proximity to the sea, the noise of people would distress her. She had buried all her family but for the two youngest. Two stillborns in a row, a dead husband, a drowned son. Finally, too, the middle boy, Simon, who at fifteen had run off to Cape Town. A year later she had been called to the Salt River morgue to identify him. Mandrax had shrivelled his skin; a pink circle from a bullet in his side.

It ceased then, that something which had been keeping her upright. Outside the morgue she could hear the terrible sound of pigeons, and beyond that there were people talking, cars moving. Buildings and streets full of people, and her child was dead. Her children, her husband, were dead. Yet all around her this terrible noise of the living was continuing.

On her return home, she did not collect Trudie and Willem from her neighbour. The next day they found her on the kitchen floor, the side of her face drooping, saliva coming from the corner of her mouth. Her chin and neck had swollen, her cheeks were hanging. From the day clinic, a volunteer came. She explained to Willem that his mother had had a stroke, that her brain and body had had a shock and might never recover. The woman showed him how to feed his mother, how to wash her and dress her. She left two adult diapers made of cloth, showing him how to bandage her pelvis into them, before fastening the points with a large safety pin.

'You must change her at least twice a day,' the volunteer warned. 'And you must feed her every time you eat – breakfast, lunch and supper.'

But there was no money for more diapers and there was no food to give her. Willem was ten years old on the day that he walked down the hill to the house of Pieter Fortuin.

Anna was afraid at the sound of the knock on the door. She had been living in Soutbek for a short time only. Through the keyhole she saw that it was a young boy. She opened the door.

'Is Pieter Fortuin here?' the boy asked.

'No.'
'When will he be back?'
'Later. I'm not sure.'
The boy looked past her into the house.
'Who are you?' she asked.
'I'm his nephew.'

When Pieter came home that night she placed his plate of food in front of him on the kitchen table and sat down opposite him.

'I thought your family was dead,' she said.
'They are.'
'Your nephew was here today.'
Pieter looked up from his plate. 'What did he want?'
'He said his mother is sick.'
'And?'
'Only that.'

Pieter did not look at her face. He brought a lamb chop up to his mouth with both hands and began chewing the meat from the bone. When he was done, he licked all ten of his fingers and returned his gaze to the plate. A potato remained next to the bones. He picked up his fork and then put it down again. He began drumming his fingers on the table. Beside his eyes small blue veins showed clearly as he frowned.

'What does he want from me? She's nothing to me. My brother married her. I can't even remember her name.'

'What are you going to do?' she asked.

'Nothing,' he said.

But later Anna heard the door close and it was a long time before he came back. In the morning she saw that there was dirt on his shoes. She ran her fingers over them; over and over, dust brittling onto the carpet. She thought of the boy, of her own brothers and sisters. Inside her something living turned over, kicking against the wall of her stomach.

The mayor entered the Cupido house and was surprised by how clean it was. He handed the packet to Willem and did not look into the dark corner where his sister-in-law and niece were asleep. He reached into his pocket and withdrew the envelope.

'I put a little extra in this month,' he said.

Willem took it. For a time the two men said nothing. Rain pattered against the plastic covering on the windows. In her sleep the old woman whimpered. A paraffin lamp stood on the makeshift table between the two men, casting shadows into slants.

'This is where you're living now? I had some trouble finding you,' the mayor said.

'It's the only place I could find.'

'I see. You understand that we can't take you in. They are going to start building again as soon as the rain stops and we have that girl for the moment and David is coming home soon you know.'

Why was he making excuses? He was doing enough already. He'd walked through the rain, for God's sake. He pointed at the corner, 'I warned my brother not to marry her. I told him to get out of here. I told him to stop fishing, to leave this place. But he was a fool. He saw what happened to our father and he learned nothing from it. I warned him. She held him here. She kept him here. She tied him to the sea and that boat so that he could never escape. And look now. He should have listened to me, done what I did.'

'What? Sell stolen goods?'

The mayor was shouting now: 'At least I did something. At least I have a roof over my head and food for my wife and can send my son to school. You're living in a hole. You have no clothes, no food! This place stinks of piss. And that wad of money you're holding in your hand, that money you accept every month, you don't mind getting that, do you? You don't have any problem with taking that! Or the food I bring you!'

Willem's lip trembled. 'The only thing he'd ever known was the sea. What did he know about farming? What did he know about the land? What did he know about anything except the sea? What could he have done?'

'What could he have done? Anything! He could have done anything! Now I sit with you and your mother hanging round my neck. This whole fucking place, all of these people, hang around my neck like a dead weight!'

He walked out of the house and back down the hill. He did not pause and when he reached his house he was out of breath, his tongue dry.

In the night the rain and wind increased. The crashing of waves and the fierceness of the storm raged without pause. Waves, higher than any remembered, hit the cliffs and shore at angles. Water sprayed and foam was churned by the constant crashing and slamming. More than a metre deep, the foam was pushed forward by the high waves, coming partly up the roads of the lower town. Everything was white with foam. There was no more shore, no link between land and sea. There was only the water: white, against dark headlands.

The mayor, despite the cool weather, lay sweating next to his wife. They did not sleep. She lay on her side, her hand under her head. Her eyes were closed and she listened to her heart beating through her ear and against her hand. She tried to ignore the storm, her husband, the warmth coming to her from his side of the bed. He lay on his back. Sweat pooled underneath him, on his forehead, under his arms and behind his knees. There seemed to be no end to the rain. There was no other season now. He felt crushed, thrown to the ground by the endlessness of it. The knowledge of what would now be expected of him was tiring, and eventually he fell asleep.

By morning there was little change. He told the townsmen to inform the people living on the beach near the factory and those whose homes would not hold against the storm that the town hall would be opened as a place of temporary shelter. He told the men to enforce the fact that there were to be no fires, toilets were to be used sanitarily, no ablutions in the bushes, and above all, it was to be understood that this was only temporary. They could not stay for good.

That entire day the inhabitants of the upper town came down the hill, sodden and cold, carrying the little they still had. Below them the foam shivered and darkened where it met the land.

Yet, within days the sun returned, the sky grew calm. Green were the great flatlands that stretched beyond the town. They looked upwards, thick with scrub.

The Establishment of van Meerman's Expedition Team

Word began to spread among the soldiers and *vryburghers* stationed at the Cape about the teams of men sent out in search of the legendary gold of Monomotapa. Excitement grew with the setting out and subsequent return of each expedition. Curiosity about the gold infected everyone, so that rumours were rife among the colonisers. Some said that the gold had already been found, but that the Compagnie was keeping it secret, not wanting to share their newly acquired wealth. Some said that the members of Everaert's expedition had located the gold and had decided not to report it to the Compagnie. Suspicions arose when they returned with one less man than they had set out with. The official report recorded Pieter Roman as having been killed during an encounter with a wild animal, but it was believed that the party of explorers had murdered him when he threatened to expose their treachery to the Compagnie. It is unsurprising that such gossip existed, for life at the Cape was not easy. The Compagnie's private soldiers laboured doggedly to build a fort that kept collapsing and found it difficult to cultivate crops that were constantly being destroyed by the wind and rain. Furthermore, many of the private soldiers were not Dutch. From as far afield as Bavaria, Portugal, France, Prussia and countless other countries, men came to join up, with the promise of adventure and wealth. However, the reality was far from what they had been led to believe, with the result that the foreign soldiers began to view the Dutch as underhanded and untrustworthy.

For the *vryburghers* life was even less agreeable. In a letter dated 30 October 1655 van Riebeeck had been given permission by the Heeren XVII to release a few men from their duties ('*in vrijdom te stellen*') and these men were granted land which they could farm. The idea was that the company could buy their produce from them at fixed prices and that the work could be done '*veel oncostelijcker*' (much cheaper). This would allow the refreshment station to become more self-sufficient. By 1658 the bulk of the *vryburghers* had entered into *boerderij* (farming) on allocated land, but there were among them also *traankokers* (whale oil distillers), *klerenmakers* (tailors), *knechte* (servants), *wiltschutten* (hunters) and a *geneesheer* (doctor).

The Compagnie supported the *vryburgher* farmers to the extent that it gave them land and replaced or repaired their ploughs for three years without cost. For the rest they were left to fend for themselves in a working environment that was harsh. Not only did the wind and rain destroy crops, but their livestock was frequently stolen by local tribes. Struggling with keeping their farms going, the *vryburghers* approached van Riebeeck in 1657 and requested permission to go on a trading mission, *'sonder Compagnies dienaers'* (without company officials) to see if *'sij van de inwoonders niet beter als met ons te samen eenich meer bestiael souden cunnen opdoen'* (without the company, we can't get more animals from the local inhabitants). However, they returned eight days later, having had slim success. After this the Heeren XVII advised that the focus of the *vryburghers* was to provide food for the sailors, not to go wandering about the interior.

By 1661 van Riebeeck was forced to admit that the situation at the Cape was so dire that *'op verre na uijt den landtbouw van haer coren tot spijse niet connen warden gevoet'* (the farming of corn and the making of bread would not feed all of the settlers). In order to feed the growing population, rice had to be imported. The more *vryburghers*, the more rice was needed. In a letter from the Heeren XVII, dated 23 August of that year, van Riebeeck was instructed to keep the number of free citizens as low as possible. As time progressed the *vryburghers* became notorious for their laziness and boorish qualities. Some among them, in order to get as much profit as they could out of their sheep, had been slaughtering them and selling them privately to individuals from ships lying in the bay. This meant that the Compagnie could not obtain enough meat to refresh the ships' supplies. The amount the Compagnie paid out to the *vryburghers* for sheep was fixed at two stivers a pound. With private sales the farmers could get double, even triple that. There were those among the *vryburghers*, too, who were selling bread at a price exceeding three stivers a pound, although the set price of one braspenningh had been established. Van Riebeeck sent out a warning: '*twelcq een schandelijcke woecker ende gansch schadelijcke uytsuyperije is, die in een wel gestelde regieringe niet magh geleden, maer ten eersten moet geweert ende g'extirpeert worden*' (this malpractice amounts to shameful usury and exceedingly harmful extortion, which cannot be tolerated in a well-ordered government, but must immediately be checked and rooted out).

After this warning, word spread among the free citizens that their land would be taken from them and they would be forced to return to military service. Military service meant hard manual labour under the Commander, strict discipline, and worse, the restriction of tight alcohol rations in order to prevent debauchery among the soldiers. Pieter van Meerman was amongst those of the *vryburghers* who knew that his days of freedom were numbered. Van Meerman had had a promising university career back in The Hague. However, drawn by a desire for adventure and riches, he had joined the VOC as a private soldier, and was one of the first to arrive at the Cape and serve under Commander van Riebeeck. It was van Meerman who was the chief instigator of the private selling of slaughtered sheep and cattle to the anchored ships. While there was no proof of his involvement, it was only a matter of time, he knew, before he was caught out or betrayed.

It happened that late one night in early February of 1662 there came a knock on the door of his homestead. Van Meerman's farm was some distance from the fort, situated in the area known today as Rondebosch. He was surprised by the knock and took care to arm himself well before answering. When he opened the door, by the light of a tallow candle, he was taken aback to find a young soldier, Jacques Fournier, a Frenchman whom he had befriended when he was still serving at the fort. Fournier was covered in blood and clutching at a sword wound on his right shoulder. He was in a state of great agitation and begged van Meerman to let him come inside. Van Meerman ushered him in and tried to give the young man some brandy to steady his nerves, but Fournier refused, shaking his head vehemently. Eventually he calmed down enough to explain to van Meerman the events of the evening which had led to this point. He and two other soldiers, Jan Brouwer and Lourens Boom, had managed to barter some gin from a sailor aboard the *Malacca* which was currently anchored in the bay. They had begun to partake of it that evening, and within hardly any time at all had emptied the flask. Jan Brouwer became increasingly loud and violent, shouting insults and curses at the top of his lungs about '*Jan Compagnie*' (soldier's slang for the VOC). When the two other men tried to subdue him, lest they get caught out and whipped for their misdemeanour, Brouwer drew his sword and began attacking them. Fournier, drunk himself, did his best to prevent the fighting, but in the fray he took a strike to the shoulder. This infuriated him to such an extent that he began swinging his sword like a madman. He told van Meerman that he could not remember what happened then, only that when he came to, Brouwer and Boom were lying dead, and he was bloodied from head to foot. Naturally such behaviour was unacceptable in the eyes of the Compagnie, and if he were caught Fournier would face certain execution. He begged van Meerman to hide him until he was able to slip away somehow.

For a number of years van Meerman had been unhappy with his lot at the Cape. The promise of wealth and adventure made by the VOC had not been fulfilled; instead his days consisted of attempting to cultivate crops in sandy soil and keep sick livestock alive. The tales of the '*goutrijcke stadt Monomotapa*' (gold-rich city of Monomotapa), and the success of the official explorers had reignited his lust for adventure. When Jacques Fournier came to him in his desperate state it seemed the perfect opportunity to embark on an expedition of their own. Fournier readily consented to the proposal. Knowing that the success of the journey would depend on numbers, van Meerman decided to recruit volunteer *'lantreysers'* (explorers) beyond himself and Fournier. There were others amongst the *vryburghers* whom he knew would be lured by promises of gold and *'de geheimen van Afrika'* (the secrets of Africa). With little difficulty he persuaded four other men to join the expedition. These were Wolfgang Heller (*wiltschutten*, a hunter), Hendrik de Jong and Barent Specx (*boeren*, farmers) and Jão Perreira (*traankoker*, a whale oil distiller). From his own *'knechte'* (servants) van Meerman recruited two men, namely Geraard van Hoesem and Isaac Rootkop. The seven men were careful to bide their time. They gathered provisions and loitered at the fort in order to collect as much information as they could about the earlier expeditions. The most challenging part of their preparations was finding a Hottentot who would be willing to accompany them as a *'tolcq'* (interpreter). It was certain that the journey could not commence without the aid of a translator, as communication with native peoples would be impossible. However, all of the translators at the Cape were in the employ of Jan Compagnie. With time, though the details are unclear, van Meerman found one of the native *'watermannen'* (water men) or *'strandlopers'* (beach walkers) who was willing to join the expedition. This man's original name has been lost over time, for to the explorers he was known only as Adam. His reason for joining the expedition is uncertain, but van Meerman suggests that Adam was fond of European delicacies such as *'brandewijn'* (brandy) and *'taback'* (tobacco). Perhaps he was bribed with the guarantee of having as much of these as he wished. Of his part in the expedition there is very little recorded, and we can only imagine what this man must have gone through, travelling with the band of mutineers.

Within two weeks of the return to the fort of the expedition under Everaert, the party of unofficial explorers had gathered all they needed for their journey. Van Meerman carried with him two quires of white paper and six lead pencils stolen from the fort. With these he kept his journal. For trade purposes they took with them several pounds of tobacco, a dozen clay pipes, three small looking-glasses, copper wire, and many beads (also stolen from the fort). The group made certain that it was well armed. They carried with them five pistols and six cutlasses, as well as eighty pounds of lead, thirty pounds of gunpowder and two bundles of fuses. The provisions they accumulated for the trip are listed below:

        60 lbs of biscuit
        30 lbs of salted pork
        4 quarts of brandy in pewter flasks
        4 quarts of Spanish wine in pewter flasks
        20 lbs of salt
        1 small bag pepper
        2 loot mace
        2 loot cloves
        2 loot nutmeg
        ¼ pound of cinnamon
        3 lbs of sugar

They also took twelve fish hooks, numerous fishing lines, two kettles and two copper pots.

Charles Geduld woke early. He and his family were living in one of the large packing floors of the fish factory, sharing with seventeen other families. It was no person or sound that had woken him, but restlessness and worry alone. Since the fire he and his wife had been given time off by the mayor to resettle before they returned to work. But they did not have the means for rebuilding their home, nor for furniture, pots and bedding. There would be no resettlement for them.

Charles stepped out of the cool building and retrieved a bicycle from what had once been the tool room. It was dirty and rusted with a seat that sat too high.

'Where are you going on that thing?' Maria asked, coming out to join him where he stood.

'I want to get some air.'

She coughed, her chest weak from the damp walls and cold floors. At night she spluttered, causing the boy, fourteen, to sigh, the girls, seven and nine, to stir. In that space were too many bodies. Sleep was difficult when others were crying, whispering, attempting intimacy. Charles mostly sat outside till late, smoking. Later he crawled in next to her, holding her quivering chest against his. The dampness of the place had affected him too, swelling his bones so that he struggled to move his fingers, or bend his knees. His grandfather chewed *buchu*, rubbing the pulp onto Charles's limbs, but no relief came. He was fifty-two and felt like an old man.

'Why don't you sit outside in the sun for a while, it will do your lungs good. I will be back soon. I just want to stretch my legs. I think some movement might help them.'

He did not tell her his plan to stop at the mayor's house. It was the garden he wanted to visit; see how it had taken the storms. Then he intended to follow the tarred road as far as he felt he could go and still manage to return. At the top of the hill he laid the bicycle on its side. Already the strain on his knees was immense and he did not wish to push it back up the incline. Gradually he walked down to the mayor's house. He entered through the gate, surveying the muddy beds, the grass too long.

Yet it had survived. Soon, he knew, there would be flowers. Just then the back door opened and out of it came the mayor's wife and the girl he had heard people speaking of. Charles stood very still. He waited quietly, watching until the women turned down the path to the beach.

Back at the top of the hill he paused for breath and lit a pipe. In the distance freighters were passing, the sun some way above them. He tried to work out the time by its progress. Past nine perhaps, getting on to ten. Then, gripping the handlebars, he pushed the bicycle through the uneven scrub to the tarred road that followed the contours of the coast. Sweat formed on his back and forehead. The road by now was mostly dry but for small indentations in which rain water still lay gathered. These he made a point of riding through, turning his head to see the pattern of his wheels worked out in damp on the black. Sheep were out on the plains, treading carefully through waterlogged, rotting land. They were muddied to their knees, enjoying the sweet leaves of the new growth. All the flatlands were moving in the sunlight, even the road was moving, black and silver in the heat.

With time, in the distance, a red shape of a car could be seen, coming nearer at great speed. Though anticipating its approach, Charles still suffered under the eruption as it passed. He staggered. Where had it come from? As far as he knew, the roads were still closed. Perhaps it was a joy rider from a nearby farm, testing the warm day. Steadying himself, he became conscious of a sound back along the road, in the direction of the car's passing. Something like a scream, though more than that. He turned the bike around, cycling back heavily.

It was a porcupine, still panting, a continuous screech coming from its snout. Quills and innards had been loosened where the car had knocked against it. Charles dropped the bike, searching beside the road for a rock. He found one and carried it back to where the porcupine lay. Using both hands, he brought it down onto the creature's head. A wet grumble came from its skull and the cavity of its mouth, splattering his trousers and wrists. He did not move the porcupine, leaving it where it lay. He wiped his hands in soil, then on his trousers. Afterwards he got onto his bike and rode back towards the town. Again the car approached, for the road went nowhere in that direction. Again the rush of its passing drove him from the road and off the bicycle, into the dirt.

They left the garden and walked towards the sea. At her beach they found the cement rectangle empty. The pot plants were gone, the bench wrenched out by the force of the waves. It now sat lodged between the rocks at the far end of the wall. Gulls settled on it and rose alternately. The wall itself was destroyed. Individual rocks lay scattered as though thrown by a great hand. Few remained now to separate beach from shore.

'Let's walk along there,' Sara said, pointing to the long shoreline. 'That looks like a nice stretch of sand.'

'I can't,' Anna replied.

'Why not?'

'My husband says... Well, he said not to walk alone.'

'But we'll be together. You won't be alone.'

'I suppose.'

She followed Sara, passing easily across the old border. Underfoot, the sand was even, scattered with pebbles rubbed smooth by waves. They walked, pocketing these, making piles out of them where they chose. Plants they did not recognise rolled in the waterline, complete with roots and leaves. Over these Sara stepped, wading out into the water. Anna hesitated to join her.

'No, it's freezing!' she laughed, her feet just covered.

Small swells shifted sand between her toes. Above her the sun burned onto her nose and cheeks, and below her, under the water, her feet were growing numb.

'Let's walk to the bend,' she said.

It did not take as long as she had imagined to reach the white cliff that marked the turn. As they came round its bow, she saw what she had always suspected: that there were other bends, on and on. But more than that, across the water, too far to be certain, there was another shore. Perhaps she would walk along the length of the sand, following the coast, until she came to that further shore. From there Soutbek would not be visible. It would not exist.

'Look here,' Sara interrupted her.

Behind them, in the pale cliff face, was a cave. Its floor was piled high with smoothed stones which they stumbled over.

'I think someone must have lived here once,' Sara said, indicating soot marks on the walls and ceiling of the cave.

'It couldn't have been very pleasant.'

'No, I suppose not.' She turned back to the mouth of the cave. 'It's not what I expected either.'

'What? The sea?'

'I thought it was supposed to be blue.'

'It's the river that makes it so brown,' Anna told her. 'The mouth is a few kilometres further up the coast and it is probably very full from all the rain.'

They returned to the shoreline, sitting in the damp sand, making piles of it with their hands, laying out the pebbles they had picked.

'And there are no palm trees,' Sara continued. 'I thought there were supposed to be palm trees. That's what it looks like in magazines: blue sea, yellow sand, warm sun.'

'I think it is that way in some places, but not here. It's never been that way here. I have never seen a blue sea.'

'If I'd known that I wouldn't have come.'

Gulls stood idly at the waterline.

She came from nothing she could put a name to. Waterless, unnatural, her home had been red heat on dust. There was nothing by which she could identify the place other than dust and heat; no distinguishing feature besides the sky, which was larger, somehow, than elsewhere. Bordered by an unsteady horizon, the sky settled on everything; hills and plains alike. Below it, the earth lay motionless. Only in the sand did creatures move, careful of the heat. Night brought with it nothing that was lush or fresh. The cold bit out, destroying what the day had not, while the moon in its slow progression watched the hopeless plains: bleached, unmoving, dead.

Out of this place Sara had grown. Not from her father, nameless, whom she had never met, nor from her mother. The sand itself had raised Sara, while her mother remained in bed each day with the windows closed, curtains drawn. The disgrace of an illegitimate child, of loving a coloured man, of being put in a car by her father and sent away, had never left Sara's mother. She swallowed down the bitterness in her throat with water that tasted of solid earth, of salt and stone and thickness.

The arrangement of life was marked only by sleep and heat. So little came out of each day, as though, dried out, they could offer nothing more. Sara became restless. She began searching through their small home, hoping to find anything of interest. Boxes came to them from time to time, with clothes, food, books, other miscellaneous items; brought by a church elder, sent by her grandmother. It was from these boxes that Sara made up her wardrobe and supplied the kitchen.

Pages of magazines, decades old, had been used to wrap a cup, a glass milk jug, a teapot. As Sara removed the covering on these items, she saw that the pages bore not only words, but pictures too: women in outdated outfits, children modelling hand-knitted cardigans. The back of one of the pages showed a long stretch of yellow sand with a bright blue sky over it. Wedged between those two colours lay the sea. Palm trees grew in the sand, their fronds reaching towards a gentle sun. Sara had read about the sea. She had known of its existence, but she had never seen it, not in pictures, not in life. The rhythm of waves, the steady flow and flow and flow of water, was something she could not imagine. She had read also about seashells carrying with them always the sound of the sea, and she tried to replicate that phenomenon by putting the hollowed-out shells of land snails in the bath for days, before lifting them up to her ear; silent, unyielding.

Returning, later, they saw a human shape moving towards them along the waterline. It was an old man, bending down and looking through the washed-up plants. At intervals he placed items in a yellow plastic shopping bag which he held in his left hand.

The two women greeted him as they passed, and Sara asked what he was doing.

'Shopping,' he replied. 'This is where I come to get my food.'

'What do you mean?'

He held out the shopping bag for them to see. Inside were tomatoes, onions and squashes he had picked up. 'When the river floods, it strips the low-lying farms and all of this is carried to me by the water.'

'But,' Anna asked, 'this can't be all you eat? You can't only live on washed-up vegetables, can you?'

The old man laughed. 'No, not always. But I've been doing it for years. My whole life.'

He looked around, determining that no one was in sight, and beckoned the women closer. 'Look here.' He reached into the pocket of his shirt, bringing out an old handkerchief. 'Today I found a treasure.'

He unwrapped the handkerchief and revealed a small round green object.

'What is it?' Anna whispered.

'A guava! It's not ripe yet, but I am going to carry it in my pocket and keep it warm until it's ready to eat!'

He wrapped the small fruit up again and returned it to its nest, patting it with pride. 'I've never found one before. It's my lucky day.'

Later still, they met the professor standing in the street near the hall. He was looking to left and right, searching.

Anna went up to him. 'Professor Pearson, have you lost something?'

'No, no. Not lost. But I was looking for someone.'

'Who was it that you were looking for? Can we help you find them?'

He eyed the people of the upper town moving in and around the town hall. They had settled by now, each finding an allotment of space within which to live.

'No,' he replied. 'I won't trouble now. Maybe later.'

'If you're sure.'

'Yes, yes!' motioning with his hands, he turned away from Anna's touch, curving to the hill.

He was disgusted by the presence of the upper towners. Yet, despite his disgust, he called them fools under his breath; fools for allowing themselves to be herded about in this way as so many cattle. Fools for living on top of one another, living in filth and promiscuity where nobody's body was their own, all things shared, all things rotting.

The man lived freely himself, using all of his rooms indiscriminately for eating, sleeping, working. Each had a worktable littered with papers, manuscripts half complete, ashtrays filled to the brim. He was working on a great treatise, a twenty-volume study of South African tribal warfare, exploring methods of attack and slaughter, political ties, regicides, conquest and battle over numerous centuries. He had begun in his thirties and many of the earlier volumes were now out of date. Entire manuscripts had been tossed aside, forcing him to start again. But the vastness of the project left him uncertain about where to begin. In all those years he had thrown away nothing, keeping notebooks, papers stacked on the floor. Some were arranged by tribe, others by decade, others by no discernible order. He brooded over the project, sitting in armchairs, smoking cigarette after cigarette that burnt down to his fingers. Already years before, he had become a laughing stock: the great professor with a magnum opus that never materialised. Why not publish each volume as he completed it, colleagues asked. What was the purpose in his waiting? But no, he would not do so. He would wait, bringing out all twenty volumes side by side in the same binding.

But the fact was that he had not written anything for years. Instead he fretted, smoking, doing nothing. And why should he? After all, was his knowledge not his own? Did it need to be noted down page after page for others to steal? At times he would write down a sentence, draw a sketch, jot down something recollected, for he read nothing now. This act forced him up from his chair, making him walk around the house. He thought over and over of the greatness of those volumes. He spoke to himself of each book as though it were already complete. Then he rushed from the house, wanting to tell of his success. But who could he tell? And, moreover, what did he have to show them? That question pained him most. He had no manuscripts, nothing written down. No. He had nothing to show yet.

The Unknown Expedition Sets Out

On 26 February 1662, in the dead of night, their provisions loaded on the backs of two pack-oxen, the expedition set out under the leadership of van Meerman in search of the *'coninghrijck'* (kingdom) of Monomotapa. They struck out northwards across the sandy plains, the cattle moaning and struggling in the dark. By dawn they had reached the *'Tijger Berg'* (Tiger Mountain) and were tiring, but since they could not be certain that the Compagnie would not send out soldiers in pursuit of them, they continued onwards. By nightfall their progress was limited as a consequence of exhaustion, and they decided to make camp on the banks of a small swampy river they had reached. However, that night the mosquitoes made so much noise and attacked the men so relentlessly, that by morning little sleep had been had and their skins were covered in bites. On 28 February they came to a place that they recognised from descriptions, a *'kopje'* (small hill) named *'Riebeeck's Casteel'* (Riebeeck's Castle) by an earlier expedition. They travelled east over the *Casteel* and shortly thereafter lost sight of *'Tafel Berg'* (Table Mountain). Finally they were able to feel secure that no search party had been sent out in pursuit of them.

The streams they encountered contained predominantly brackish water and the weather was oppressively hot. Dysentery, caused by the salty water, was rife among the men. This was aggravated by the heat, which made travelling during the afternoon unbearable. Jão Perreira suffered the most. Crippled by dysentery, he kept falling behind. Towards late afternoon on 1 March, it was brought to van Meerman's attention that Perreira was missing. Wolfgang Heller and Isaac Rootkop were sent to look for him, while the rest of the men built a fire to guide him, as it was already getting late. All through the night there was no sign of the men, and the cackling of *'wolven'* (wolves, or rather hyenas) was chillingly close. The next morning Heller and Rootkop emerged through the scrub, carrying

Perreira between them, having spent a terrifying night in the dark. On that day the explorers managed only an hour's journeying, for Perreira was too ill to walk and had to be carried. Realising that it would be in the best interests of everyone if they let Perreira recover, van Meerman ordered the men to make camp for the next few days. During this time the men saw many '*vogelstruysen*' (ostriches) and '*paarden*' (zebras). Heller shot a hartebeest, parts of which the men roasted over the fire. Slowly, with rest and care, Perreira began to improve.

In the days that the men were camped in this area, Hendrik de Jong kept to himself. He shied away from company and did not join the conversations of the other men around the fire. On the last night of their stay at that particular camp, the explorers had heard the roaring of lions and had even seen the glinting of eyes in the firelight. In the dead of night, despite his proximity to the fire, de Jong was dragged from his sleeping mat by a lion. Though de Jong made no sound, van Meerman had been wakened by the beast's panting and growling. He jumped up, calling out and waving. The lion dropped the man and fled. De Jong lay where he was, unmoving. When van Meerman reached him, he saw that de Jong was alive, his eyes were open and he was expressionless. Van Meerman helped him up and led him back to the fire. The composure of the man amazed him, and he asked how it was that he had made no call for help. At this query de Jong began to sob, whispering at intervals that he wished to die. Van Meerman was astounded at this revelation, and poured the man a double ration of brandy, sitting with him until he calmed down. After some time de Jong had regained enough self-control to explain his behaviour. Fitjie, the girl he had loved ever since he was a young boy, had married him and agreed to come and live at the Cape with him. Though life was difficult, for two years they had lived happily together. When she fell pregnant in the winter of 1661, she was incredibly ill. One evening, a few months later, he came home from the lands to find her moaning on the floor, with blood pouring from between her legs. There were no neighbours within shouting distance and he did not wish to leave her alone for the two hours it would take to go to the fort and return with a doctor. With no knowledge of what his wife was going through, de Jong tried to nurse her as best he could. Yet the following morning she was dead, and the baby, its legs sticking out from her body, was dead too, smothered in the birth canal. He blamed himself for bringing her to this place which was *'eenzaam en naar'* (lonely and terrible). She had been good and kind and beautiful and had deserved a better life than the one he had brought her to. He hated himself for what had happened to her and he wanted to die. There was nothing for him to live for. He had only agreed to come on the expedition because he had hoped that it would be the death of him. He confessed to van Meerman that when the lion had grabbed him he had felt that finally he would be at peace, but the other man's interference had robbed him of that release. It seems that eventually de Jong fell asleep. No more mention is made of this incident throughout the journal, and it can only be assumed that van Meerman kept the information to himself.

In the days that followed, it began to rain and travel became difficult. When they got to the Bergh River it was so swollen that the men wasted a full day in floating their possessions across. They camped on the opposite bank of this *'claere revier'* (clear river) and ate fish in abundance. To the west they spotted a large herd of hartebeest. Van Meerman and Adam went in pursuit of the herd in the hope of catching one for their dinner. As they were passing a mound of rocks, Adam suddenly called out, *'Bijteman, bijteman*!' (A biter, a biter!). Looking up, van Meerman saw a lion which was making straight for him. He had little time to react, but fortunately he kept his wits and managed to aim well with his firearm, hitting the lion in its chest. Adam thought it might have been the same lion that had dragged de Jong from his bed and that it had probably been hunting them for days. Van Meerman took the time to cut off the furry tip of the lion's tail, to keep as a souvenir and show to the other men.

Strengthened by the fresh food and rest, the men continued their journey after a few days. Van Meerman's success with the lion had renewed their morale and they began talking about themselves as *'couragieuse manne'* (courageous men). Restored to their original focus of the quest for gold, the men sang as they travelled:

> *Ik zi het ingewandder hoge Bergen zoekken,*
> *Op hoop van puyk Metaal. Den Hottentoo verbaast,*
> *Di sidderd ende lild, ja sgynd de Tyd te vloekken,*
> *Om dat ons Donder-bus tot lof van Holland raast.*
> *Men trekt te Landwaards in doorsnuff'lend alle hoekken,*
> *Men vind een beter Aard' van Mensgen, stel u sgrap,*
> *Man-moedig Neer-lands volk, gy vind door lang te soekken,*
> *Gy hebt u 's Heeren wensg, dat's puyk van Koopmansgap.*

I see the settler searching the high mountains,
In the hope of precious metal. The Hottentot is amazed,
He shakes and trembles, cursing Time, powerless,
Because our guns fire for the glory of Holland.
Explore the interior, search all corners,
Find a better type of person, prepare yourself,
Courageous Dutch nation, through long searching
You will have God's wish: a prosperous expedition.

In the days of heat that followed, the flooding river finally began to recede. Bridges and roads became visible again, and with time teams of workers began to clear the mud and debris. Where bridges had been washed away, repair work became a priority, and farm roads across private land were opened, allowing people to reach those places which had been inaccessible.

Soon delivery trucks came to Soutbek. Heavy with fresh eggs and milk, bread, meat, fruit and vegetables, their wheels trembled in the drying mud. In the store the shelves and fridges were restocked; cupboards in homes stood full. The mayor ordered large amounts of fresh food on his own account, which he presented to the ladies who ran the soup kitchen to distribute as they saw fit. Each day now soup and bread was accompanied by two pieces of fruit. The members of the upper town ate them sitting on pavements, standing in the street. They wiped their hands on their clothes and threw pips and cores into gutters, where gulls fought for the remains. In their homes, behind their doors and walls, residents of the lower town tore into apples and peaches, tomatoes and cucumbers they had bought with their own money. They ate without plates, without knives or forks, enjoying only the feel of something fresh in their hands, of juice running down their chins. Their hunger was not the same as those from the upper town; only the knowledge that they had been deprived, that they might have suffered had they been poor, drove them to such behaviour. Yet amongst themselves they spoke with disgust about the manners of the upper towners, shaking their heads, clicking their tongues.

Small donations were sent by charity organisations from neighbouring towns. Downpours and flooding had wrecked their own rural communities; there was little left to share. From the wealthy metropolis of Cape Town nothing came, despite appeals. Similar storms had ravaged the Cape Flats, and it was beyond their already stretched resources to consider a distant town of a thousand inhabitants, when hundreds of thousands were suffering in the sandy plains of the Flats. Nothing could be spared.

As though a reminder of an untroubled life, flowers came after the rain. Over-run, the scrublands lengthened, a band of colours, pink, orange, blue, stretching out of sight. Unsure of how to behave or dress, people came out of their houses. In the days of rain they had longed for heat, and now they found themselves uncertain. Only fragments remained in their memories of what heat was, of sun and the outdoors. They dressed in cardigans and jackets, wore scarves and vests, sweating under their weight, unwilling to take them off. Men and women alike ventured out into the flatlands. They picked flowers for their kitchen tables and night stands. Acclimatising to the weather, they spoke more, laughed more, and from the town hall people erupted. Laden with bundles of clothes they had washed in the bathroom sinks, women came out into the streets, hanging their clothing on bushes and fences, or made their way down to the Mayor's Wife's Beach where they draped shirts and dresses over rocks. The women stood in groups near their laundry, heads wrapped in scarves. They spoke loudly, about the fire and the storm, their homes, their children. What would become of them? they asked each other, reciting their complaints one by one. They shook their heads, made the sign of the cross, and said they would remember each other in their prayers. But in their hearts there was no room for pity for others. For each woman her own family was all-consuming.

Around the country *The History of Soutbek* was having enormous success. The weekend paper published an article, two pages across. Included were pictures and biographies of the authors. Further articles and interviews followed in other newspapers. Three PhD students chose to include the work in their theses, reviews began to appear in literary journals, and several university history departments placed the book on their students' recommended reading lists. The text itself was examined for quotes. These were taken out of context, and used to champion disparate causes nationwide. Some condemned the work; many applauded it.

With the book's growing popularity came a demand for the authors. Both the mayor and the professor were invited for interviews or to speak at symposiums and literary events. Night after night the two men sat together to prepare. The professor rehearsed the mayor in those questions which he anticipated. But the mayor could retain nothing. He listened and wrote down and repeated, but still the answers would not remain in his head. He was stunned by their success. All this time he had waited, and now to find himself the author of a book 'magnificent beyond its modest claims' was something for which he had had no preparation. He was struck by his own philanthropy. See what he had done for the town! In his dreaming he allowed for his success to range the globe, his name on everyone's lips.

The professor did not suffer under the same bewilderment as the mayor. In public he fielded the bulk of the questions, protecting as far as he could. Under the gaze of so many, that old and foul-smelling man became erudite and witty. Where the mayor could speak only of Soutbek, of the wonder of the town, the professor spoke of history. He brought people face to face with their ancestors. Through *The History* he showed them a past they could be proud of.

'I am a servant of history,' he told them. 'I serve it.'

He believed this of himself, having adopted the notion early in his university career. Ill-health as a child had left him unwilling to accept weakness of any sort in his later life. He had been self-possessed, confident, seeing the map of his future before him. He made no allowance for failure and chose a route which would guarantee success. He understood that in South Africa there existed a need which had to be met, and he knew that he could fulfil that function. Extensive funding, as well as a successful career, was assured him if the outcome of his postgraduate research would confirm certain ideas. The nature of the research, with its conclusion already worked out for him, held a guarantee of success. He would serve this conclusion, making it true, changing the world with his findings.

During the years in which he worked on his research, Terence retreated further into himself. He read more and more about the tribes which the early settlers at the Cape had encountered. Records showed how the tribes were constantly fighting and cheating one another. The result of his research was inevitable: a fierce defence of the actions of the South African government's institution of Apartheid. History, he argued, proved that it was necessary to keep different peoples apart. It was evident that there could be no peaceful co-existence, not among tribes, and not between settlers and tribes. In conclusion, he argued that for Apartheid to be most successful, it would need to be carried further, with peoples from each individual tribe being located in respective areas or camps across the country, no interaction allowed.

For a number of years Terence was a leading academic voice. But with time both worldwide and national disapproval mounted. He found it increasingly difficult to have his papers published in journals, or to be taken seriously in academic circles. Students walked out of his lectures, his house was attacked with rotten eggs and fruit. He found dog shit in his pigeon hole and graffiti on his office door. Towards the end he was barely teaching, publishing nothing. He was told that there was no longer room for his kind of thinking at the university.

The professor did not disdain the person he had become. He felt no remorse for his actions. He believed that what he had done was fair and just. He had rendered a service and been paid for that service. He had moulded the past into a suitable present, giving people historical proof of what they already believed.

With the passing months the homes on the hill began to be repaired, and a few of the families moved back to the upper town. Gardens were started again, with flowerbeds delineated by broken gutters and worn tyres, decorated with seashells. In various streets old men brought chairs and radios outside, turning the volume up, so that hymns from the gospel station filled the air. Children played in the dust, running barefoot, bare-chested. The smell of the sea was strong, and from the northwest came the scent of plants and the sound of bleating lambs. In the evenings the sun set later and later, forming red and gold patterns on the sea. The inhabitants stood outside their shacks and watched, hungry. After dark some ate in secret, ashamed of what they had and their unwillingness to share. Later, when the town was dim and invisible, the only sound was the creaking of tin roofs, shrinking in the cool air blown from the sea.

Drunks became a common sight in the upper town. Few fishing boats had survived the final storm, and the men, their days empty, sought solace where it could be found. They sat on the sloop, watching the sea with resentment, wondering how they would provide for their families. Their skins felt dry on the land. They walked in the dust of the roads, staring in dismay at the imprint of their shoes behind them. Their children were eating soup and bread once a day. What could they do? At night they stared at fly-blown photographs of parents and grandparents which had been preserved from the fire. They knew no other life. There was for them only the sea. Outside their homes, fishing nets were strung between posts, serving as washing lines.

Driven by boredom the men came together in groups of five or six in the dusty area above the sloop. They dug small holes in the ground, collected stones from the dirt and played games they had not thought of since they were children. It was a game they ill-remembered, having to make up new rules so that differing versions developed amongst the individual teams. Into the holes they had dug, they emptied out the collected stones, making attempts to grab them back between the throwing into the air and catching of a larger stone. They argued over the fine points; the process of the game, whether it was allowed to grab more than one stone at a time in the first round, or whether all were removed and one less returned. They scrabbled in the dirt, yet in their playing they forgot their troubles, turned to children again.

Around them, with newspapers borrowed or found, others read aloud about the success of the mayor and professor. They had seen them in their finery, driving off to various appointments, and heard of their fame. Understanding little of it, they wanted to read for themselves what had happened to cause this sudden change. The reading was a protracted event, suffering many interruptions. Listeners laughed as the reader stumbled over words, or if he was too inept they called for a change, not bothering to spare any man's feelings. They cut short the flow with queries about what certain phrases meant, or they wandered off to watch the players in the dirt, needing to be updated upon their return. But Charles's grandfather, the oldest man present at eighty-seven, said nothing, leaning on his stick, squinting against the glare of the sun off the water. There was not a thing he did not know about the bay, the cliffs, the plains, and he listened carefully. From time to time he pinched his nose, with fingers gnarled in places where nets had cut them. The man felt his age now, walking slowly, thinking slowly and talking in the same delayed manner. He waited until the reader had finished before he said, 'They don't know what they're talking about.'

'What do you mean, Oom Bekkie?' they asked.

He hemmed, spitting at the dirt beside his feet, 'They know nothing about Soutbek. Not as it is, not as it was. Maybe I don't know much, but I've lived here for many years, my whole life, every day, never been anywhere else, never will, and I never heard anything about this before. Never heard about this group of explorers.'

'But *Oom*,' they protested, 'that's the point. It's new information. No one knew it before.'

The old man stood still for a time, taking in the houses, the flatlands behind them. Then he turned slowly and shielded his eyes with his hand, as though searching for an answer on the waves. Eventually he spoke. 'No, I never heard a thing about it, not once. It isn't true.'

He spat one more time and walked away unhurriedly towards a rock, on which he sat, his hat over his eyes.

Days slipped by in this fashion, and more and more a wish to return to life as it had been came to those of both the upper and lower town. In the lower town the inhabitants were tiring of the noise, the litter. They had come here to retire; they had come for peace and quiet. Could the soup kitchen not be moved? they asked. Could the people not get on with it and make new homes and get out of the town hall? The mayor heard their complaints. He was doing his best, he said. He would see what he could do, but it wasn't easy. They didn't care: there was no space for these people in the lower town.

Those from the upper town, in turn, felt discouraged by their growing dependence on the lower town. They needed its soup kitchen, the protection of the town hall. They wanted to leave, but where else could they go where there would be roofs over their heads, running water, free electricity? It was impossible.

NAMAQUA

On the afternoon of 15 March the men had just began to unload the oxen in order to make camp for the night when they sighted a *'rhenoster'* (rhinoceros) coming towards them. They knew of the fearsome tempers of these creatures and, fearing for the safety of their oxen, the men rushed towards it, armed with guns. Their confrontational tactics did not work, for the animal continued coming forward. Heller and Fournier took aim, and though their shots were true, the bullets could not pierce the thick skin of the *rhenoster*. As the animal continued stampeding towards them, in the mad rush of shouting and firing and running, de Jong was tossed into the air by the *rhenoster*'s horn, before being trampled under its feet. Running forward, Heller, the *wiltschutten*, managed to shoot the beast in the eye, at which point it sank to the ground. The men then attacked it with their cutlasses, piercing its thick skin until it lay dead. Though de Jong was still breathing after his ordeal, his injuries were grave. He died in the night and was buried the next morning. It seems strange that, in the light of his conversation with de Jong on the night he was dragged from his bed by the lion, van Meerman simply recorded the episode leading to his death, without making any further comments. In any event, the group was depleted by one, and though this meant more provisions were available to each man, their troubles soon increased.

As water sources became scarcer, so was there *'schraelheijt der weijde'* (lack of grazing) for the oxen. On the morning of 22 March one of the oxen refused to get up. It was exhausted, had an infected hoof, and was not getting enough food. The men had no other choice but to kill it. They spent half a day digging a grave in which to bury the dead beast as they did not want to attract more lions to their trail. When they packed up their belongings each man's already heavy load was doubled. In the days that followed there was much dissent among the men. They were unhappy about the extra loads, increased by the deaths of both ox and man. Progress was dreadfully slow and the men were exhausted after every step. Geraard van Hoesem and Barent Specx were the loudest of the complainers. Specx was notorious as far away as his native Holland for his boorish behaviour. He had joined the VOC only as a means of avoiding the law, for he was wanted for various misdemeanours in the homeland. At the Cape he was known to have stolen livestock and crops from other *vryburghers*, using the war with the Khoikhoi as an easy way of laying the blame elsewhere. Van Hoesem, angered by a hostile environment, spurred on by Specx during the journey, became rebellious and offensive. Uncouth and filthy men both, they complained at full volume not only about the heavy loads, but about the lack of water, van Meerman's leadership and the compass direction the group was taking. They wanted to travel towards the east, while the rest wanted to continue as they were in a north-northwesterly direction. After several days of belligerence, Specx and van Hoesem said they could no longer agree to stay with the party and would be setting out on their own. Van Meerman agreed to this with great relief, and willingly shared out to them their portion of the supplies. The two mutineers took their leave towards the east. Of these men nothing was ever seen or heard again, neither in van Meerman's journal nor in other records.

It is after this episode that the journal begins to cease recording dates. Based on descriptions of weather, stars and plants it is at times possible to estimate the season, but no exact dates can be pinpointed.

It was also after the leave-taking of Specx and van Hoesem that the party's luck began to change. Van Meerman does not record many of the details of the events of the next few days, but it appears that somehow they met a handful of Grigriqua who bartered them a bag of honey for tobacco. These men, when questioned about the Spiritu Sancto, replied that they knew of a great river and they would take them there. It was not too long before they came to a large river. The men were amazed by the presence of up to 150 elephants on the opposite bank.

Remembering what had happened to poor de Jong with the rhinoceros, the men kept their distance, opting to remain on the south bank until the elephants moved on, despite the bemused urgings of the Grigriqua. This was certainly the Oliphants River reported by the previous expeditions. The company was quite exhausted and it seems to have taken them a further two days to get to the Grigriqua *kraal*. During that time they did not see a trace of water anywhere and van Meerman commented about the '*groote armoede*' (great poverty) of the land.

From information pilfered from the fort before their departure, the men had discovered that they should travel towards the Namaqua, since it was believed that this tribe was in amicable trade with the cities of Monomotapa. Van Meerman and his men were pleased to find that the Grigriqua were allies of the Namaqua. That evening the party of travellers had a feast held in their honour. They shared out some of their depleting supply of alcohol and handed out pipes with tobacco, walking around the circle of people seated around the fire, showing them how to suck on the clay pipes. It took some time before they could get any of the Grigriqua to agree to take them to the Namaqua for by this stage they were drunk and raucous, unused as they were to alcohol. But the following morning they set out, and it appears not to have been too many days later that the Grigriqua called out, 'Namaqua!'

Van Meerman's record of his time spent with the Namaqua is not always credible. There are numerous anomalies in the text; various customs or behaviours which are better understood as van Meerman's own interpretations rather than actual facts. But it is certain that he took the time to try and find out as much as he could about the Namaqua, and it is many of these investigations into their life and culture which are found recorded in this portion of his journal. There is evidence that van Meerman attempted to learn some of the Namaqua language, which he, disparagingly, recorded as follows after his initial encounter with them: '*hun sprake gaet geduurigh met klokken, als de kalkoensche hanen, klappende, of klatzende over het ander woort op hun mont'* (their speech is filled with constant clicks, like turkeys cackling over each successive word in their mouth). Yet, despite this critical view of the language and documenting that he found it tended towards the monosyllabic, van Meerman struggled to learn anything beyond a few simple words and phrases. He understood the usefulness of learning their language so that he could communicate without a translator, but years in the service of the VOC had instilled within him their policy, whereby native peoples were expected to learn Dutch, not the other way round. In fact, a fellow soldier, George Frederick Wreede, had compiled the first Hottentot–Dutch dictionary, which had been brought to the Heeren XVII. In his work, Wreede had allocated various symbols to indicate the many different types of 'click-sounds' used by the Hottentot peoples in their speech. He was the first man to make a linguistic study of their language. The Heeren XVII had congratulated Wreede on his work and ingenuity, but had rejected the dictionary, on the basis that it was not in accord with their policy.

Van Meerman indicates that after encountering the Namaqua scouts, the expedition was led to their *kraal* by men well armed with bows, arrows and assegais. They also bore shields so large that a man could hide behind one. The Namaqua *kraal* took the form of a large circle which was enclosed in a great fence of thorn bushes. In the fence were two gateways, one facing north, one south. Within the fence there were about sixty-five huts belonging to the '*!Haus*' (tribe). Each *kraal* was host to a number of patrilineal sibs, meaning groups of people who are related in the male line. One of those sibs claims seniority and it is within that sib that the chieftainship is inherited along the male line. The following is the order of the sibs in the *kraal* as recorded by van Meerman: in the western portion of the *kraal*, facing east stood the huts belonging to the chief's sib. To the left of the chief's sib, facing east, came in order the *!Oa Gaon*, the *//Naigaman*, the *!Gurusin*, the */Gari Karin*, the *!Neise-ein*. To the right of the chief's sib came the *Goamun*, the *//Khau*

Tanasen, the /Gari Gein and the !Ga ei Tanasen, which met the !Neise-ein in the east of the *kraal*. Outside the *kraal* there were three huts which were occupied by men who had no cattle. They acted as messengers for the chief between himself and other tribes. The cattle were herded into the open space at the centre of the *kraal* at night. Calves and lambs were kept in separate *kraals*, but the cattle or sheep would simply sleep in front of their owner's hut. The contents of each hut were sparse. They consisted on the whole of '/garu-ti' (sleeping mats), '//hoe-ti' (milk vessels), cooking utensils and ostrich eggs. Van Meerman was most impressed by the sight of their '*karosses*' (shawls of animal skin) for those Khoikhoi who lived around the Cape fort wore their skins uncured. He took it as a sign of the Namaqua people's civilisation.

When the explorers were led into the *kraal*, they were brought before chief Akembie. Van Meerman had warned the men to keep an eye out for '*costelycheyt*' (riches) such as gold, copper and pearls. This they had no difficulty in doing, for the people were all richly adorned with many beads and other ornamentation of copper and iron. Chains with copper discs suspended from them were wound some fifteen or sixteen times around their necks. On their arms were rings of copper and ivory. Flat pieces of ivory hung over their genitalia. Their legs were adorned with plaited thongs studded with copper beads. Some even had their hair threaded with beads.

The explorers were advised to address the chief as '*gouaob*' (fat man) or '*!khu-aob*' (rich man). These were customary terms for rulers and were used interchangeably, since a rich man could afford to be fat and to anoint himself with '*goub*' (animal fat). Akembie was seated on a chair studded with copper beads, draped in skins also studded with copper beads. They were astonished to find that upon his head there was a '*roo mutsen*' (red cap) of the Compagnie's soldier's uniform. Others of the leading men who stood near the chief also '*die roode mutsen hadden*' (had the red caps). Akembie greeted the men and asked them their business. Van Meerman explained that they were simply travellers who were exploring the land. He said that their intentions were friendly and asked Adam to teach Akembie the phrase *'onse vrindt'* (our friend). On hearing that, Akembie welcomed them to the *kraal* and asked if they had brought more gifts, for the last white men had given them many, including the red caps they now wore. Van Meerman replied that they had many gifts, but no red caps, for they were not part of the other white men's company. They were on their own and not tied to the fort at the Cape. Upon hearing this information, Akembie began to frown and stroke his red cap. Van Meerman asked his men to begin unpacking their gifts of tobacco, beads and brandy before the chief, but Akembie continued to look displeased. Eventually van Meerman remembered that Fournier still had the orange sash from his soldier's uniform and asked him to present that to the chief. Immediately Akembie looked better pleased. He draped the sash across him and invited the visitors to stay with them as long as they wished.

The explorers were given two huts in which they could stay and were invited to a feast to be held in their honour that night. The men gratefully accepted, but explained that Perreira would have to be excused as he was not well. Plagued with dysentery, he had been ill for days. Akembie nodded wisely and said that it happened from drinking brackish water that the blood entered the stool. He sent one of the medicine men of the tribe to care for Perreira. He was given wild figs for the dysentery and *buchu* was used to cleanse and heal a festering blister he had developed on his heel.

That evening a fanfare was blown. About 150 of the Namaqua men formed a circle, with each man holding a hollowed reed, some of which were long, others short, some thick and others thin. In the middle of the circle one man stood holding a staff and singing, while the others blew on their reeds, dancing in a circle. The women danced around the outside of the circle. They feasted on honeybeer, grasshoppers, fruit, buttermilk, mutton and beef. This went on for some six hours until the travellers could barely keep their eyes open, and were forced to retire.

Over time the riverbed separating the upper and lower town had eroded into a gully bound by rocks. The ground here was low and marshy, covered in *suurvye* and weeds of different types. Though a road existed connecting the two parts of the town, many took short cuts through this gully. A path through the vegetation had been tramped clear. Sara made a habit of stepping off the track and walking deeper into the gully. The place was secluded and cool, untouched by the heat of the levels above. This time, having veered too far from the path, she had been compelled to make her way down by means of the rocks. It had been a difficult descent and when she reached the shade below, she sat down, leaning her back against the cool stone. But for the sound of cars nearing and distancing overhead, there was quiet all around. Dust had filtered in at the edges of her shoes. There were marks on her ankles where she had kicked herself in stepping down. She began rubbing at these smudges, tempted to take off the shoes altogether.

She thought of Willem. He had spoken to her three times only since finding her in the kitchen, despite his tendency to be often nearby. Twice she had nodded at him, receiving an 'Afternoon' from him as they passed each other in the street. The third time she had been standing in the garden as he came in, asking for the mayor, and she had had to remind him that he was in Cape Town for the next two days. He asked how she was. She answered that she was fine. Then she had excused herself, apprehension of him making her behave in that way. Just recently she had seen him nowhere. His absence increased her anxiety, waiting for sight of him again. She had heard from Anna about his troubles: the mad mother, a sister. Despite her fear of him, she admired him, beginning to mention him in her prayers each night. Not prayers as such, but a list of names to be remembered.

Just then she looked up the slopes of the channel. Above her, close by, stood Willem. He was looking at her, partly smiling, partly licking his lips in the heat. He waved hurriedly, having taken off his cap. His hair had been cut, leaving it shorn close to the scalp where before there had been dark curls.

'Having a rest?' he asked, climbing down from the rocks.

She nodded, looking at a scratch on her middle finger, her eyes away from his.

He sighed and sat down beside her. She shifted uneasily. Since her arrival in the town she had filled out, gaining breasts where there had been none. Now, in his presence she became aware of them, embarrassed.

'You've had a haircut, I see,' she said quietly, hardly looking as she spoke.

He laughed, rubbing his head with his left hand. 'It's my summer shear. It gets too hot to have as much hair as I had.'

She was silent again.

'I have a lot on my mind right now,' he said. 'There is a lot to be thinking about, a lot I need to be doing.'

'I know.'

She wished he would leave. For days she had watched for him, looking for his shadow where there was none and now he was here and she wanted him gone. Beside her he continued to talk and she only just heard his question, 'You must feel sorry for us? The way we live in the upper town?'

'It's not for me to say.'

'But you wouldn't want to live like us? Would you?'

'I don't know. I suppose not.'

He nodded in agreement. 'You see.'

The knowledge of the poor's dependence on charity had sat heavily with him since the mayor's visit to the Cupido house. There were people he loved in the upper town and others he didn't care for at all. Still, he felt the cruelty of the situation that they all shared. The mayor had told him the book would improve things. There had been no proof of this claim yet.

In small numbers tourists began to appear: middle-aged couples on West Coast bird-watching excursions, carloads of international students in exchange programmes at universities in the metropolis. They were, without exception, disappointed by what they saw. Was this the historic utopia they had read about?

The mayor watched their reactions from his office, seeing in their expressions a reflection of his own dissatisfaction. It was not enough simply to have written a book. The work amounted to too little. If he wanted tourists to come then substantial changes were required. The physical make-up of the town had to be altered; houses for the homeless, for a start, and then accommodation and a restaurant for sightseers. He would need an information bureau – that could be fitted in alongside the town hall – and pamphlets, in colour, with activities and sights to take in – such as what, for God's sake? But he refused to occupy himself with the details just then. Patience had no place now. He had come to believe in the ease of success, made more so by his demand for it. Here was the land, the sea all around him, exhausted by his father, his grandfather, his brother. It was this that he had inherited, and it was his to renew.

With so much on his mind, the mayor neglected other responsibilities. Each morning he told himself to phone social services about the girl, but each day he forgot, and the yellow reminder note beside his office telephone began to fade in the sun. He was busy, too busy, to sit for hours trying to organise such things. But perhaps because these days he saw in his wife's face softer lines, a warmth around her mouth and eyes that he had not seen before, he ignored the note with purpose. The mayor forgot too about the additions to his house, leaving rooms unfinished. He had other, more pressing projects in mind for the builders, which he hoped to begin soon.

LIFE AMONG THE NAMAQUA

In the days that followed, the explorers began to feel stronger and well fed. As guests to the *kraal*, they did no work, and so they spent their days sitting in the sun outside their huts, watching the activity going on around them. They slept much of the time, for they were still tired from their journey, and the luxury of having nothing to do soon encouraged laziness. It became common practice that some of the senior men of the tribe would come and join the men outside their huts to partake in tobacco and brandy. The explorers had not forgotten their search for the wealthy Monomotapa, and so they continuously asked the Namaqua elders the origin of their '*ǂei*' (copper) and '*/urib*' (iron). These questions the Namaqua pretended not to understand, or answered evasively. Van Meerman and his men determined that it would take some time to win the tribe's complete trust.

A week after their arrival at the *kraal*, van Meerman caught a Namaqua man in his hut, trying to steal the last of their Spanish wine. Furious, he took the man to the chief, who reprimanded the man soundly and told van Meerman, '*Khoikhoi tamab, Sab ke*' (He is no Khoikhoi, he is Sa). This is as much as saying, 'He is no gentleman [Khoikhoi meaning men of men], he is of low extraction or a rascal.' Akembie said that he had had much trouble with this man, named !Guŋbee, for he did not wish to do any work and was insubordinate. However, not wanting to cause trouble, van Meerman requested that the man go unpunished, and that he be given another chance. Akembie agreed to this, saying that van Meerman had the makings of a great chief, for the worst thing a chief could be was '*gei-//are*' (greatly left-handed or stingy).

After this, !Guŋbee became devoted to van Meerman. He followed the Dutch man wherever he went, and began sitting at the edge of the circle of elders which formed around van Meerman each day. With time it appears that the two men became friends, and van Meerman found !Guŋbee to be a bright and entertaining man. !Guŋbee was soon able to converse in broken Dutch, and explained to van Meerman that he was looked down upon by his fellow tribesmen because he had no cattle. The Dutchman replied that he understood well what !Guŋbee's situation was, for he himself had come from a place where he was looked down upon for having little.

The two men sat together most days, talking and waiting for the women to bring them food. Mostly the women brought 'χ*urina*' which is the collective word for roots, berries, honey and bulbs gathered in the veld. Van Meerman developed a taste for the '*!naras*' fruit, a type of melon the size of a newborn baby's head. The custom was to eat the flesh raw and then keep the seeds to be eaten in the dry season. He ate these seeds by the handful, claiming that they tasted much like almonds. Steadily, van Meerman and his men could feel their stomachs expanding and their bodies filling out.

Among the women who brought the travellers food every day was a girl named !Urisis. Van Meerman was utterly spellbound by this girl with her nut-brown skin, round breasts and dark eyes which she lowered every time she came before him. He began concocting errands she could run for him, merely to spend some time in the happy anticipation of her company. He would ask her to take gifts of tobacco and beads to the chief and she would always reply, '*Goreb !na ta ni tani*' (I will carry it in the palm of my hand). His agitation whenever !Urisis came to his hut was evident, and the old Namaqua men would laugh at him, for they knew the signs of love, which were the same in all men no matter what their colour. Van Meerman asked !Guŋbee about the girl and was told that she was the daughter of Akembie's son, !Urisib, who had died in a battle with the Numaqua a number of years before. The old men, sitting nearby, teased van Meerman and asked him why he was so curious about this girl, and he replied that there was no reason. '*Heitse!*' they warned him. 'She may have a body like a cow's body now [that is, a beautiful, fine, fat body], but look out because a woman cannot be quiet for as long as it takes sweet milk to turn sour! And once you're married, *Heitse*!, you get scolded all day long. You can't even put your hand in the food pot without getting shouted at!'

It seems that after some time, at van Meerman's request, !Guŋbee approached Akembie and asked what van Meerman should do in order to be granted !Urisis's hand in marriage. Akembie's reply was that she was '*Gei khoits õase*' (a great man's daughter) and therefore she could not be married to a man who owned no cattle other than a single pack ox which was barely alive. No, he could not let it happen. Van Meerman was devastated by the news and began to brood.

Devoted to the Dutchman and seeing that both van Meerman and !Urisis were '*//ã//ōs*' (dying of love), !Guŋbee went to the girl's uncle, Xam/hab, and begged for his assistance. Xam/hab agreed to supply van Meerman with '*disi go-ma-i*' (ten cattle), as well as with the meat for the wedding feast. Akembie was not very pleased at this turn of events, complaining, '*!Goahe tamata ha*' (I am not counted, meaning, I am unfairly treated). He accused Xam/hab of trying to make him, Akembie, look like an ungenerous chief, when all he was doing was protecting the traditions of his tribe and caring for the future of his granddaughter. After much arguing and deliberation it was decided that Akembie and Xam/hab would each give van Meerman ten head of cattle, on condition that the cattle were to be kept with their own herds.

When van Meerman heard what Xam/hab had done for him with the help of !Guŋbee he was overjoyed and shared out the last of his tobacco with the two men. His fellow explorers were less pleased, however, and Jacques Fournier took him aside to remind him of the real aim of their mission. Yes, they understood lust, but to actually marry this '*vuil prinsesje*' (dirty princess) was another thing altogether. Embarrassed by what love had done to him, van Meerman explained to Fournier that the marriage was simply a ploy for getting into the good books of Akembie and finding out the location of their copper and other treasures. Fournier, Rootkop, Perreira and Heller were disgruntled, but agreed to trust their leader. Adam, on the other hand, had grown tired of life among the Namaqua and missed his own people. After the brandy and tobacco ran out he decided to return to the Cape. Without a word, he left one night.

In preparation for the wedding many cows and ewes were slaughtered. The explorers were informed that tradition held that no other livestock could be killed in that time as this would mean the couple would have an unhappy life together. Van Meerman and the others had to participate in ceremonies along with young Namaqua men. The fattest cow was found and then chased around the *kraal* as the young men beat it with sticks and stones, encouraged by the shouts of others. !Guŋbee explained to van Meerman that tradition states that the cow should become so tired that she will stand still, trembling with fear, and allow herself to be touched. However this cow was a spirited one and she continued to kick and fight with the men. At this a great cry rose up among the people. Van Meerman asked what was wrong and !Guŋbee explained that the cow's continued fighting signified the continued fighting of husband and wife. To this another man added that it would be particularly bad for van Meerman for he had heard that !Urisis' mother had eaten leopard meat when she was pregnant, which meant that her daughter would bear that creature's violent characteristics. Van Meerman shrugged his shoulders and smiled, but !Urisis looked away, her eyes downcast.

!Guŋbee told van Meerman to look closely at the heads of the goats in the days leading up to the feast, for if they shook their heads and wagged their ears then it was believed that it would rain, which was crucial for the newly married woman. She must run in the rain and let it cover her whole body so that she will be fertile. No such shaking occurred and so the rain makers were called. They sprinkled their urine into a burning fire and cut their fingernails and also threw them into the fire. After that they caught a bird known as '*ǂgã//goeb*' and burned the bird to ashes. These ceremonies succeeded in bringing the rain.

Van Meerman recorded that he was taught a song which he was expected to sing to his bride at the wedding feast. It went like this:

> *Ti xamse !*
> *!Gaibista !aote ?*
> *Gomasa ke /ausi //gain !omsai !*
> *Natere !*
> *!Gabe-/khatere !*
> *Ti xamse !*
> *Gei khoits oase !*

> My lioness!
> Are you afraid that I will bewitch you?
> You milk the cow with a fleshy hand (that is, with a soft hand)!
> Bite me! (that is, kiss me!)
> Pour for me (milk)!
> My lioness!
> Great man's daughter!

These were amongst the last of the happy days that the explorers spent with the Namaqua.

The two women walked out over the plains, which were turning browner every day in the heat. They picked the last of the wild flowers. A haze had covered the flatlands, giving the distance a dreary look, the sky a colour monotonous. After some time they halted in their walking, pausing to watch the freighters of ore passing on the raised tracks beyond, each woman counting to herself the number of carriages that made up the chain.

'Two hundred and fourteen,' Sara said.

'I had two hundred and seventeen,' Anna replied.

Without comment, they watched the freighters pass from view, becoming aware in the silence of the gentle vibration of the telephone wires nearby. A small hawk, perched on the wire, sat watching them.

'Later they will come back this way,' Anna said. 'You get to know the marks on some of the containers and then you can watch them travel back and forth.'

Sara looked at the woman beside her. Such a small life; dirt under her nails, a walk on the beach. 'Aren't there other things to do?' she asked.

'Not really.'

'But what about that book? That one everyone is talking about.'

'You mean the history book?'

'Yes. What does it say about this place?'

Anna shrugged. 'I'm not sure; I haven't read it.'

'Why not?'

'I can't.'

'You can't read?' Sara asked.

'I can read words, short sentences. Enough, but not a whole book.'

'Doesn't your husband mind?'

'He doesn't need me to read.'

'And he hasn't told you what the book is about or read parts of it to you?'

'He doesn't have time to do that. He did tell me about it. Well, he told me that it was the history of this area and it would bring money to the town.'

'Why don't we read it?' Sara said. 'I will help you. We'll do it together.'

The other woman glanced up, about to speak, when from far away in the still afternoon came a strange sound that neither of them immediately recognised. Grabbing the flowers they had picked, they ran across the flatland in the direction of the road. In the distance they saw a van with a red flashing light. It was not moving very fast, and as it neared, the siren getting louder, they realised that it was an ambulance. So slow was its approach that they were able to make out every detail of the occupants. One man, the driver, had a moustache, a cap that seemed to be splitting at the brim. He wore a gold chain around his neck and an earring in each lobe. The other was smoking, tuning the radio, it seemed, with his right hand. As the ambulance passed, he stuck his head out of the window, making a loud lip-smacking sound at the two women. They stepped back from the road. Watched the lazy movement as it turned off onto the dirt track that led to the upper town, its shape vanishing amongst the burnt houses.

In the evening Willem interrupted their dinner. The mayor did not invite him to join them, simply gestured with his knife that he should say what he had come to say. Willem explained that the ambulance had come for a five-year-old girl who had been feverish for days.

'This morning she began throwing up and said her neck was stiff.'

The mayor reached over to a bowl of pumpkin on the table before him, dishing out more onto his plate. 'So she's at the hospital, is she? I'll send sweets tomorrow. Just remind me. Maybe also some flowers for the family.'

Willem shifted where he stood. 'She isn't at the hospital. The ambulance was out when her father phoned. It took too long to get here.'

The mayor stood up, throwing his fork onto the table. 'Are you telling me she died?'

Willem nodded.

'That's all I need,' the mayor said, leaving the room.

The story of the little girl's death brought to mind Anna's own family; their bare feet and laden backs. She had no way of knowing what had happened to her brothers and sisters and felt certain that she would not recognise them if she were ever to meet them again. The deaths, she knew, of some of them were probable. She wondered where they had been buried, and how. In her dreams the corpses of her young siblings walked past her, faceless.

On the day of the little girl's funeral, the memory of her family drove Anna up the hill and through the channel to the dirt roads of the upper town. She had never been there before and did not know her way around. She followed the sound of hymns, coming eventually to the church with its low bell tower, the cemetery beside. She did not enter the church where the mourners were, nor did she pass through the gate of the cemetery. Instead, she remained where she was, standing outside the fence, watching as the mourners left the church for the graveside. They did not wear black, for many of them had only the clothes on their backs. But the few who still had them wore hats, and the drawn faces were all clean, as were the hands and nails of those who picked up fistfuls of dirt and sprinkled them onto the coffin. Afterwards, they stayed beside the grave without words. They made no haste, feeling somehow accountable for the many that were absent. Despair had kept them away; the small grave too resonant of their own futures. Loss encouraged them ever more to drink.

Later, when only Willem remained, filling in the grave, Anna came forward from behind the fence.

'What can be done?' she asked him.

'There's no need,' he replied. 'Your husband has already paid for all of it.'

She had not been speaking of money, but at the mention of her husband she looked around. 'He's not here, is he?'

'No. But he paid for it,' he replied as he shovelled.

'All of it?'

'A proper casket, an actual headstone, engraved. They will deliver it next week. Friday, I think.'

'I didn't know.'

'It will mean a lot to the family, the headstone. There are so few who can find the graves of their dead.'

Night was falling by the time she returned to the lower town. Pieter sat in the dark lounge, watching the news. The light of the television reflected off his face and she saw in it something of what she had known before.

'Where have you been?' he asked.

'I went for a walk.'

'You know what I said about that. It's dangerous.'

'Sorry.'

Anna stayed with him as he watched TV. He was tired, dozing most of the time, his hand twitching where it had fallen to his lap. That night, Anna allowed her feet to brush against his in her sleep.

Despite the onset of summer, the Gedulds had had no word from the mayor about returning to work. Charles had spoken to him several times. Each time the man had been distracted, unwilling to give an answer. He encouraged them to enjoy their holiday while they were able to.

Bound by nothing, Charles became used to resting all day. He sat in the sun outside the fish factory. He played the stone games of his youth. He dozed. His wife saw his ease and was careful not to let him know how much pain she was in. They barely spoke now, having only their troubles to speak of. And she cried sometimes when alone, reluctant to tell him what she feared he did not already know: that she could not return to work. She wanted to ask him what would become of them, how they would survive. But he had turned blunt, comfortless. He was never happy now, nor tender. Not cross even, only matter of fact, listing their troubles as easily as counting.

When the swelling of his joints grew worse, he was compelled to attend the day clinic sometimes held in the upper town. After examination, he was advised to continue with the *buchu* compresses made for him by his grandfather, but he was warned that there would be no change until he had a warm bed away from the damp. Even then his recovery would be partial. He could not work, certainly not with his hands, and it was better to avoid using his legs too much.

The need for money became even more immediate then. He needed a house. He needed to get himself and his family out of the factory before the following winter, before his hands ceased functioning altogether. Work was the only solution. He went to the lower town, and found the mayor away. Instead he spoke to Anna. She apologised for the delay.

'It's not up to me, you see. But I will tell him when he gets back and I am sure he will let you know very soon,' she said, before enquiring after Maria, the children, his grandfather. She gave him fruit from the bowl on the kitchen table and a packet of rice from the pantry, careful not to stare at the claws his hands had become. On the doorsteps of other houses he visited, he held his hands behind his back. It made him look suspicious, overly confident. They locked their doors to him, tired of the sight of beggars.

Charles returned to the sloop. He sat on an upturned crate, unable to crouch in the dirt any longer. He knew he was not alone in his situation, but he felt that he was. He alone had been strong once. He alone had become an old man. There was nothing for him now. He was used up.

He had ugly moods in which he hated Maria, his family. He might have gone away when the fish factory had closed. He might have done something else with himself. Instead he had got stuck digging up the gardens of others. Finding in their soil artefacts he had no claim to. A shard from a tea cup. A rusted tin in which rested the skeleton of a long-dead rodent. Bulbs that would never again grow. The soil belonged to the mayor, as did its contents.

In the evenings, after dinner, the two women brought out *The History*, taking advantage of the mayor's absences to read it together. They sat at the kitchen table, going slowly through each sentence. They reread individual paragraphs, making certain they understood. With the Dutch words they laughed at their pronunciation, grateful for the included translations. There was no haste in their reading; they returned to sections they had liked, discussing the use of certain words, using a dictionary when unsure. Willem found them in this fashion one evening. It was Sara he had come to see, though he had no reason for his intrusion that he could speak out loud. He surprised them and they flushed when he entered. They had not heard his knock.

'Oh, it's you,' Anna smiled. 'Sara is helping me with my reading.' She held up the book for him to see.

Willem had not bothered reading the copy given him by the mayor. Despite what the mayor had told him, he did not believe that a book could change things for the people of Soutbek. Few in the upper town could read well enough to have any interest in reading for pleasure. The town had only a primary school, with no transport to the high school two towns away. Whatever the book might say, if no one could read it, it was meaningless. But he was encouraged by the opportunity to spend time with Sara and asked if he might join their reading group. 'I have my own copy. You wouldn't need to share.'

For some time now the idea of the girl had been with him continually. He had only to close his eyes and he could see her as clearly as if she sat in his palm. In his remembering of her he exaggerated her beauty. He added shades and curves where there were none. That night, after they had agreed to his joining their reading group, he went home wanting only to impress her. He read by candlelight, practising sections of the book in advance, searching for words that he could stumble over, so that she would turn her head towards him, as he had seen her do with Anna, whispering, 'Good, good.'

For Anna, not only the reading of *The History*, but *The History* itself became a pleasure. 'This is wonderful,' she kept saying to Sara and Willem. To her husband she said the same each time she was near him, though he did not hear her, for she never said it out loud. She had grown to admire him once more. His kindness to the family whose little girl had died, his kindness to Willem, the wonderful history he had recorded; it all added up to someone extraordinary.

She read and reread the description of de Jong's encounter with the lion. Often she cried at the poor man's self-loathing for bringing his wife to such a desolate place. But she was ashamed of her tears, too ashamed even to wipe them away, so that she sat shaking her head. Sara would hold her at these times, surprised at the end when Anna smiled, asking if they might read just a bit more before bed.

The Search for Gold Continues

In the weeks that followed the wedding, van Meerman became increasingly interested in certain aspects of the Namaqua way of life; particularly those aspects of Namaqua culture which concerned the Namaqua's relationship with snakes. When a hunting party returned to the *kraal*, carrying a man who had been bitten by a snake on his foot, van Meerman watched as they bound the leg tightly at two places under the knee in order to prevent the poison spreading. They then cut the foot and covered it with fresh cow dung that was still warm. After that one of the Namaqua men bent down and sucked the blood from where they had cut him, spitting it out onto the ground. Van Meerman was amazed at the swiftness of the man's recovery and the lack of pain he experienced.

Shortly thereafter van Meerman was privy to another incident involving a snake. A young girl ran screaming through the *kraal* explaining that she had seen '*!Ganin-!gub*' while she was milking the cows. The '*!Ganin-!gub*' is a type of snake that the Namaqua believe to possess genitals with which it attempts to impregnate girls. The full tribe was compelled to stay up for the entire night, singing and dancing, in order to drive away the fiend.

After these two experiences, van Meerman let it be known throughout the *kraal* that he would offer beads and tobacco for large snakes if they were brought to him alive. He was not wholly certain what he would do with them once he had obtained them, but his curiosity was piqued, and he was growing bored of being idle all day. The following morning a young man came to him and opened his kaross, showing two yellow cobras coiled around his arms. Van Meerman brushed tobacco oil onto their mouths and noses, causing them to become unconscious, whereupon he placed them in a jar for later inspection.

That evening one of the cobras escaped from its jar. Van Meerman immediately grasped his pistol and shot at the beast as it was making straight for him. He shot the snake in its neck and in her agony she flung herself a distance of more than thirty yards across the centre of the *kraal*. It was after this event that van Meerman began to notice that he was treated differently. People would say '*!gai-aob ke, !gai-aob ke*' (He is a sorcerer, he is a sorcerer) when he walked past, and avoided his eyes.

Alienated and uncertain, van Meerman grew anxious, for the Namaqua had begun to talk about migrating north for greener grazing land, before the winter rains trapped them and prevented their passage. His fellow explorers also grew uneasy. They were no nearer to finding Monomotapa and had no wish to follow the Namaqua herds aimlessly. In addition, the situation at the *kraal* was becoming tense, for the novelty of the visitors had worn off. Their idleness was annoying the Namaqua, who complained that the '*!uri-au*' (white man) was '*/hobe*' (lazy).

As tempers began to rise a terrible event happened which confirmed the fate of the explorers. Again the incident involved a snake. Isaac Rootkop had gone to bathe in a nearby stream. The Namaqua believed that in each fountain lives a snake called '*ǂGãbeb*' (the one who lives in a hole) and if the snake leaves the fountain or dies, the fountain will dry up. It so happened that on the day when Rootkop arrived at the stream, he found it to be dry. As he approached the dry bed, he disturbed a cobra, which reared at him, ready to attack. In order to protect himself, Rootkop picked up a stone and brought it down on the cobra's head. At that same moment several women appeared, come to fill their water jugs. When they saw what he had done they ran back to the *kraal* to tell Akembie that one of the white men had killed *ǂGãbeb* and that there was now no more water.

As a consequence of his actions, despite explanations, Rootkop was banished from the *kraal*. Knowing that the other members of his party would go where Rootkop went, and realising that his own relationship with the Namaqua was disintegrating, van Meerman was in turmoil. Could he drag his new wife away from her family? He remembered the story of Hendrik de Jong's wife, who had died in labour, and he felt ill.

That night, sitting outside his hut, smoking with !Guŋbee, van Meerman was told a tale which interested him greatly. !Guŋbee pointed at a cluster of stars and related their story, which van Meerman later recorded:

> The */Khunuseti* (we know these as the Pleiades) said to their husband, 'Go and shoot those three Zebras for us; but if you fail, don't dare to come home.'
>
> The husband went out with only one arrow, and when he shot, he missed. He sat where he was because his arrow had missed. On the other side stood the Lion watching the Zebras, and therefore the man could not go and pick up his arrow to shoot again. Because his wives had cursed him he could not return home and therefore he sat in the cold night shivering and suffering from thirst and hunger.

From scribblings in the margins of his journal at this time, it appears that !Guŋbee's tale resonated with van Meerman. Though faded and torn, one can make out the following on the left-hand edge of the one hundred forty-third page of the manuscript:

Paarden (zebras) = *Monomotapa*
Man (husband) = *ik* (me)

Consequently, one can construe that van Meerman interpreted this piece of Namaqua star-lore as a personal allegory, whereby the failure to shoot the zebras echoed his failure at reaching Monomotapa, and that his future with the Namaqua would be like sitting out in the cold. It is this tale therefore, we the authors believe, which finally decided van Meerman in favour of leaving the Namaqua camp. The following morning he approached Akembie and struck a bargain. He agreed that in return for the information he had requested regarding the origin of their treasure he and his men would depart, leaving behind the generously bestowed wedding present of cattle. Eager to rid himself of the explorers, Akembie fabricated a position for the precious metals in the area near the big river where the elephants were.

While the rest of his party readied their belongings, van Meerman (as he is at pains to point out in his journal) encouraged !Urisis to remain with her family. But his wife was with child, as well as deeply in love, and therefore chose to leave the *kraal* and all her family behind, becoming the sole woman in the band of white explorers. She was, however, not the only Namaqua to join the explorers, for !Guŋbee too had elected to leave the tribe where he had no standing, and chose to join the white men, where there was a position waiting to be filled, that of *tolcq*.

Akembie was furious at the news that two of his people were leaving. '*!Goahe tamata ha, !Goahe tamata ha*' (I am not counted, I am not counted) he shouted over and over. Those were the last words the party heard as they left the Namaqua and travelled back towards the Oliphants River.

The salary of a mayor of a small town was slight. Pieter continued with those acquaintances with whom he had had dealings in the past. He kept a hand in selling stolen merchandise, investing the profits by buying properties in Soutbek and Genot. Where he could, he purchased stocks and shares. After realising what adjustments were needed in order to turn the town into a viable tourist destination, the mayor phoned his financial adviser, telling him to begin the process of selling his stock and properties. Next he began to undertake those steps required for updating the town's facilities.

'I have business in Genot tomorrow,' the mayor told his wife. 'You can shop while I'm busy, and then we can meet David at the bus depot.'

'David?'

'He's coming home for the holidays. Did you forget?'

Anna had not imagined his return from school would be so soon.

'Sara...' she said.

'She will have to stay behind. There won't be enough space in the car, what with the shopping and David's luggage.'

But what she had meant was, 'Sara is enough. I don't want the boy.'

In the two days before their marriage, Pieter had kept his distance. He did not touch her in any way, paying for separate rooms where they spent the nights. But when she climbed into the car after the small civil ceremony, wearing her new dress and shoes, he had laid his hand on her thigh. Except for changing gears, he did not remove his hand. It was oversized on her small thigh, the knuckles dark and hairy. She tried to crawl out from under it, pushing her neck into the seatbelt.

He told her about the house he had bought. It was small, he said, but bigger than anything she would be used to. It had a kitchen, a lounge, a bedroom and an inside bathroom. It had a front garden, and at the back, a washing line. They drove through the afternoon and it was night by the time they arrived at Soutbek. She could not make out the sea. Before them was only the dark of the road lit up by the car's headlights, and shadowy expanses on all sides, which might have been anything at all.

Inside the house he had led her to the bedroom. He placed her small bag in the corner and told her she looked tired. She should get into bed, he would be back soon. She undressed and climbed under the covers. She did not know which part of the house he had gone to. She could not hear him and was almost asleep by the time he returned, naked, silhouetted by the passage light. She had not noticed his girth before. Now the belly and chest, the swirls of his nipples, the dark trembling of his penis, were strange to her. He climbed into bed, filling the space beside and above her, groping at her breasts, his tongue on her face. His body pushed against hers, trying to get in, and then a voice, clear, very clear, saying there was a problem. He lifted the covers, and taking each thigh, pushed her legs wide apart. Next he leaned his head between her legs and spat into her before raising himself above her and pushing against her again. This time the resistance was torn, and afterwards when she went to the bathroom she found blood on her thighs.

By intervals his body became less alien, the daily intercourse less painful. But still she felt that what she had known before, what she had believed, had been false. Since the day she had left the farm, there was in him nothing she found familiar. She learned to remove herself from the events of intimacy. Too soon her period vanished and she came to understand that she was pregnant. She thought of the being inside her as a strange amphibian creature with webbed limbs and a lipless mouth. When it was finally born, covered in blood and mucus, it was as though she were being handed her own internal organs in a blanket. She had turned away and refused to look at the child for days afterwards.

Driving to Genot with her husband, Anna watched as they passed along flat land covered in low scrub; sweeps of farmland, with grazing sheep, no houses in sight. The road ran straight ahead of them, continuing on and on, so that it felt to Anna as though the clouds came no closer, the distance remained distant. But then the grazing land gave way to vineyards, packed neatly along the course of the river. Farm labourers walked through the rows, picking bunches from the knotted vines. Along the river, beyond the vineyards, trees grew, heavy with the nests of weaver birds. On the other side of the river, clear of the trees, the same could be seen, more vines, more workers picking grapes.

'A few months ago this was all flooded,' her husband said, pointing. 'They say the vines have never looked so good. It must be all the silt.'

'Is this the river where the explorers saw the elephants?' she asked.

He looked at her in surprise. 'Yes. A whole herd of them.'

'A hundred and fifty of them I think it was.'

'Something like that.'

Nearing the town, the ruins of old farmhouses could be seen, and further away, new houses, large and white. The road dipped so that without warning before them, above them, were vast grey uprights, high up, metres and metres high, supporting the train tracks over the river.

'Are those the same tracks that run past Soutbek?' she asked.

'The same.'

'But they're so high!'

'They put them high up because of when the river floods.'

'But so high?'

'It was built in the 1920s. There was a lot more water back then.'

The streets of Genot were wide and flat. It was the largest town in the district, with some 14,000 inhabitants. On Saturday mornings everyone that was able from the outlying farms and small towns made their way there. Main Road, the business portion of town, was the most crowded. As her husband drove through the slow-moving traffic, Anna looked out at the busy street. *Bakkies*, brown with dust from farm roads, were packed high with groceries and lined the way. There were men on horses, too lazy to drive, cutting past delivery trucks that had stopped in the middle of the road. Others, on bicycles, dodged the traffic, wedging themselves in where they could. Dogs sat in cars and barked at the activity. Nearby on lamp-posts hung tabloid headlines marked out in yellow board for all to see. In the windows of grocery stores maize meal was advertised beside promises from the store to be a friend to everyone in hard times. Upon the pavement was continuous movement. Many farm labourers and their families loitered outside the liquor store and budget supermarket at the top end of the street. A woman with a *doek* on her head, wearing a paper crown, swayed from side to side in the parking lot. Livid, shrivelled, she shook her hips, crying out, *'Ek's die Queen van Genot! Ek's die Queen van Genot.'* Her neighbours laughed and pointed, *'Ou Queenie, ja! Wys o's Queenie!'* She smiled and waved, did a half-curtsy before reaching under her skirt to pull down her panties. Then she hunched down, pissing, all the while saying, *'Ek's die Queen,'* but softer now, as though she might fall asleep where she crouched.

Anna remembered her own trips into town as a child. Though the town had been smaller than Genot, she was able to recognise the clean morning expressions of faces washed with soap and water over a hand basin, the swaggers of people wearing their town clothes. Beyond that she recognised, too, the hard lines and slow walk of people tired after a week's labour. Women and children stood on corners and in the shade with grocery bags. The walk back to their respective farms, she knew, would be long and heavy. Already there were drunks in the streets, both men and women. They shouted and staggered, repeating their behaviour from previous weeks. She thought of the signs of the *Plaaswag* she had seen on the way to Genot. A yellow and red triangle with a silhouette of a farmer wielding a shotgun: warnings to labourers and others that the crops were guarded, the houses of farmers protected.

Beside her, the mayor changed gear, his hand jerking on the lever, eyes fixed on the road. Anna shifted slightly, bringing her leg closer to him. He stopped outside a small shopping centre. Farmer's wives, fat, sat in a coffee shop, talking loudly, while opposite, outside the Agrimark, the men stood at their *bakkies* smoking. Anna stepped out from the car and the mayor placed several notes in her hand. 'I'll be back to fetch you at three.'

Like the streets, the aisles of the grocery store were wide. The same fat women pushed laden trolleys and gossiped with the tellers. Anna needed nothing. She bought a few toiletry items for Sara, food for Willem and his family. Afterwards she walked through the centre, passing slowly from shop to shop, waiting. At the window display of a small jewellery store, she paused, seeing a pair of silver cufflinks, inlaid with ivory. For several minutes she stood looking at them.

'They are antique. Probably around 1890,' the sales assistant told her when she enquired about them.

'They're beautiful.'

'Made in England, but the ivory is from an African elephant. That's before ivory was illegal to trade in.'

It was impossible to know whether the ivory came from one of the elephants that had lived in the region before. Herds of them had been hunted and killed across the continent. But in her own mind, Anna allowed herself to believe that what she held in her hand had once been part of an elephant from the Oliphants River; those same elephants she had tried to imagine walking through the vineyards along the way.

When the mayor returned for Anna, he placed her shopping bags in the boot of the car. The cufflinks, wrapped in a small box, remained in her handbag. He drove to the bus depot on the outskirts of town and parked. While they waited for David's bus to arrive, he got out of the car to make a phone call. Anna remained seated, only half-listening to his voice, 'Vernon, you owe me. I know you can help me with this.'

A movement on the grassy verge next to the car caught her eye. She turned her head and looked out of the side window. It had come from a bird, a black bird with a white breast, perched on a stone. She tried to recall whether it was a crow or a raven that had the white breast. Something hung from the bird's beak and she smiled, thinking it a worm. She watched her husband continue to pace, talking quietly now. On the verge the bird continued tugging, and she turned to look at it again. 'Crow,' she thought, mouthing the word, at that same moment realising that it was not a worm hanging from the bird's beak. It was not a worm at all. Nor was it a stone on which the crow was perched. It was a head; the head of a dog. There was no other part of the dog's body, simply the head, its tongue hanging out, its neck ragged. The bird sat on that head, pulling strings of flesh from its neck. Anna turned her face away and looked into her lap, pressing her hands together over the handbag. She could hear her husband's voice, the sound of buses moving, and in her mind the image of that dog.

She heard her husband open the door. 'He's here.'

Anna thought she might fall. She let herself climb out of the car slowly, careful to avoid looking at the verge. She walked around the car and glanced up. From where she stood she could see the boy. Was he that young? And yet he was older, clearly older, and her insides shifted at the sight of that dark mass of hair, his round face, neat clothes, his arm reached up in a wave. In her mind there was only the dog's head, its ragged neck. She felt unsteady on her feet and clutched at her husband's arm with both of hers. He, startled by this movement, showed it with a warm glow on his face. She was light, so light, and he felt that he was carrying her across the street, lifting her over the pavement and gutter.

When they came to the boy, she did not let go of her husband's arm as she bent down to greet him. Reaching her closed mouth towards the boy's cheek, her own against his, her nose leaning towards his neck, she felt ill. There was a smell of travel, of heat about him. He was raw and rotting. She saw before her the neck of the dog.

They drove back as they had come. The boy talked about school, his friends, rugby and cricket. In the front seat Anna thought about the fact that for the nights to come her son's breath would be in the same house as her again. It would travel up the passage, through rooms and rooms, until it came to her; a fist down her throat, squeezing.

On their return they found Willem and Sara in the kitchen, *The History* unopened before them. The two had been sitting like that for some time, speaking of other books, books they had read as children. The girl mentioned titles he had never heard of, books with dusty covers that she had found in boxes, their language archaic. Willem had to think hard to recall the books of his primary school, wrapped in brown paper and plastic to protect them. There had been many stories about a brother and a sister who ate jelly and played with a dog, and a book he only half-remembered, set in another country a long time ago. In that story families had sailed from across the seas, penniless, their children dying on the voyage. Once they had reached the new land, they travelled by ox-wagon, living in canvas tents, searching for gold in long, waterless plains. It was a book he had found in the small school library, a book without pictures. He had abandoned it unfinished. In repeating to Sara those few details he remembered, he felt that he understood it better now, having read in *The History* something similar. 'The search for a better life,' he had been saying as Anna walked in. 'We were waiting for you before we started,' he explained.

'Started what?' asked the mayor, coming in with David behind him.

Sara pointed to the book on the table. 'We're reading this.'

The mayor grunted, 'Well you can't do it now. David is here. He's tired and we need to eat.'

Beside her child Anna looked uneasy, holding on to the back of a chair, turned away from him.

'He'll have to leave,' the mayor added, inclining his head towards Willem.

Sara watched without comment as Willem rose from the chair. 'Get a good night's sleep,' the mayor said. 'I have a job for you to do, starting tomorrow.'

Willem said nothing. He lifted his jacket from the table, reaching each of his arms into a sleeve. He walked towards the door, pushing past the boy, feeling shamed in front of Sara.

'You don't want the job?' the mayor asked. 'I can easily find someone else who will be only too glad of the opportunity in these difficult times...'

'No, I'll do it.'

'Well, good. Seven o'clock then, at my office.'

Willem did not go home. He remained outside the mayor's house, watching the shadow movements behind curtains, slow actions of people making dinner, eating, getting ready for bed. In the night every sound was bare; the turning of a tap, the rush of water into a basin, cupboards opening and closing. He saw Sara step out across the yard to her room as the mayor locked the back door. After that he waited for the lights to be switched off, for the house to become still. His footsteps seeming loud in all that quiet, he walked across to the door of the outside room and tapped softly. From inside came her voice, 'Who is it?'

'Me, Willem.'

She opened the door, wearing a nightgown that stretched tight across her shoulders. Her hair was wet and he could see the slope of her bare neck, her arms. Water dripped from her hair.

'Can I come in?'

'It's late.'

'I thought we could talk some more,' he said, putting his hands in his pockets.

'I'm going to sleep soon.'

'Just for a while, please,' he said. 'Please.'

Sara stepped aside and he walked in, turning in the doorway to where she stood, still holding the door. He could smell the heaviness of damp hair, and the sharpness of toothpaste about her. He bent his head to her neck, kissing it. She did not move. Her neck was warm against his lips and that warmth travelled through his skin, into his mouth, so that he brought it up to hers, his hands gripping her waist, pulling her towards him. At first they kissed as they had seen others kiss, the motion awkward. But soon they felt sure enough to move freely, and laying her down on the bed, he felt confident enough to kiss her feet, her calves, her back.

Later he drew her towards him, kissing her forehead, 'Can I help you clean up? I've heard there's blood the first time.'

Sara allowed him to strip the sheet from the bed and lead her into the bathroom, where they stood together, naked. He carefully wiped her thighs, cleaned between her legs. Then he washed the sheet in the bath, scrubbing the patch of blood with his knuckles. When he went home, Sara lay on the bare mattress, feeling the remains of the warm oval their bodies had left.

In the early morning, mist was coming in from the sea. The cliffs and beach were invisible in the thick air. On walls and roofs throughout the town drops of condensation were forming, leaving everything damp and heavy. Willem knocked on the door to the mayor's office. Despite having had little sleep, he felt good and found the mayor in a similar mood.

'Good morning, good morning,' he said, standing up from behind his desk and discarding the documents he had been reading. He gestured at the window, smiling. 'You will have noticed that we're getting a lot of tourists now. We need to make the town a more pleasant place, more inviting, you understand?'

'How do we do that?' Willem asked.

'Yes, I'm getting to that right now. We need to make an overall good impression. I am already organising some very exciting improvements, but one way that we can get started is by giving the town a few coats of paint.'

Willem blinked. 'The whole town?'

The mayor laughed. 'Obviously we can't do it all, not the private properties. Anyway, those are mostly pretty well kept so they are not a problem. But we can do the public buildings and the houses that I own and go from there.'

He led Willem to a store room at the back of the town hall. Inside were hundreds of tins of paint.

'Where did you get so many?' Willem asked.

'An old friend knows someone and gave me a special deal.'

'Stolen?'

'I didn't say that.'

Willem sighed. 'What do you want me to paint?'

The mayor pointed through the doorway of the storeroom. 'You can start with the town hall and then move on to the benches and fences.'

'You want me to paint the town hall?' Willem asked.

'Yes. That's first and then as I said the...'

'But it was painted eight months ago. I painted it myself.'

'And now you are going to paint it again,' the mayor replied, walking away.

After laying down plastic sheets around the base of the south wall of the building, Willem fetched a tin of paint and some rollers. Using an old screwdriver he prised the lid off. The paint inside was thin and grey. According to the label it should have been sea green in colour, but inside there was only a dull watery substance. He took a stick and stirred, thinking the colour and bulk had sunk to the bottom, but still when he poured it into a paint tray it was pale, almost clear. The roller did not immediately pick up the colour, so he tried again, before swiping it across the white wall. He stood back and waited, seeing the grey paling further as it dried. After a few minutes, he licked his finger and ran it across the streak of paint. It came away easily; the wall white as before underneath.

Willem fetched the mayor from his office. 'You can see it's too thin. It's like watercolour. As soon as the mist comes in it will wash off. We can't use it.'

The mayor's good mood was gone. 'Don't be ridiculous. I have a thousand litres of the stuff. You have to use it. Keep painting, just do layers.'

'I'll need ten layers to make an impression and even then it will wash away.'

'I don't care. Just paint the fucking place.'

This Willem did, each day revisiting the same wall, painting and repainting, only to return the next day to begin again.

David woke to find he had missed breakfast. There were dirty dishes on the table, the house was empty. On the countertop he found the key to the outside room and let himself in. Underwear lay on the floor, there were dishes on the bed, dust on the bedside table, a bin overflowing with tissues. His mother's clothes were bundled into the cupboard alongside a wet towel and more dishes. In the bathroom the toilet was not flushed. The boy went back to the kitchen, getting himself a bowl of cereal, which he ate lying on Sara's bed. Afterwards he locked the door behind him, leaving the bowl amongst the clutter.

Next he walked down to his mother's beach. Plastic cups, foil sacks from box-wine, paper plates and more littered the sand. The pot plants were gone; his mother's bench hung between two rocks, metres out to sea. All around, the stone wall had been destroyed and youths from the upper town leaned against the ruined perimeter, smoking. As he straightened up from looking at the two grooves where the bench had been ripped out, David saw the approach of Charles from across the shingle. Even from that distance he could see that the man had changed in the intervening months and that he moved now with difficulty. As a young child David had spent much time with Charles, playing alongside him in the garden. They had been very fond of one another, but that had been years ago, yet still the man held an annoying idea of them being friends. He made a pest of himself when David came home for the holidays, bringing him presents, toys made from tin and knuckle bone, inviting him to walk out into the veld.

'There you are, *kleinbaasie*,' Charles called out.

David waved, hoping to leave it at that.

'I'm coming,' the old man cried. 'Just a minute till I get there.'

The boy was impatient to be gone. 'I must be going home. My mother doesn't know I am here.'

'One minute and I'll be there, don't you panic,' Charles replied.

David could have gone to meet him, instead of waiting as the old man painfully made his way up the small incline to the cement square.

'Now, don't you worry about your mother. She knows you're safe when you're with me.'

He looked up the road wildly. 'But she doesn't know I'm with you.'

'My God, you've grown. Such a long time since we last saw you. How are you, my boy?' He reached out his hand, extending two fingers that the boy shook gingerly.

'Fine, thanks.'

'I hoped to see you here. I only just heard this morning from Willem that you were back and I knew you'd be worrying about us after the fire, though that's quite a long time ago now, but anyway I had to come and say hello.'

'Yes.'

'You're getting taller, and more handsome. Just like my Gershwin, you remember him? You saw him once, remember, it was many years ago, but I'm sure you will remember, he and I were walking along the road and you and your pa drove past and we waved at you. You wouldn't recognise him at all now, he's grown so much. He'll be fourteen soon. Exactly two months after your birthday. Almost like twins, Maria and I always said.'

'How is she? When is she coming back?'

'Oh, I don't know. She is a bit sick just now. A bit sick in her chest, you know. But that's just what I wanted to talk to you about, you see. Won't you do me a favour and remind your dad about us? Tell him I miss the garden, tell him that I am ready to come back. He's been so busy. I don't blame him, but if you can only remind him about us. Say we miss the garden, you know.'

'I'm sorry, it really has nothing to do with me. You must talk to him yourself,' the boy said, stepping away slightly.

But Charles had rehearsed this all morning. 'Do you remember, now tell me if you don't, but I can't see how that can be, do you remember when we went driving to Genot, you and me and your dad? We were driving along happy as anything and then you started screaming there in the front seat, because there was a big black mamba in the road. Huge, do you remember? And "Papa, Papa," you said, "Don't drive over it!" And your dad had to stop and old Charles had to get out and push it off the road with a stick before you would let us carry on.'

'It was a long time ago.'

'I remember it often. Anastacia was just a baby, Jaydene not even born yet. I still tell that story. The day the *kleinbaasie* screamed for us to rescue a mamba.'

Just then a loud group of young men emerged from the town hall, and David took the opportunity to say, 'I really must go now.'

'Of course, *kleinbaasie,* but you will have a word with your father for me, won't you? A word for your old friend.'

'I'll tell him I saw you.'

'Yes, tell him your old friend must come back, you miss him.'

As David walked away from the beach the youths called to him, thick-accented words he did not understand, and he looked away, down at the dirty sand and shells, brown with urine. Nearby lay a pile of faeces, fly-blown, human. He walked faster, ignoring the calls behind him.

Walking through the lower town, he became aware of how much had altered. Women from the upper town stood talking to one another on pavements and in the road; a group of children begged outside the store; and more children, dozens, were running through the streets. How could his father allow such devastation? He had taught David determination, taught him to take what he wanted and never wait to receive. So why had he allowed this to happen? Why was Willem in their house, why was a homeless girl eating at their table, wearing his mother's clothes and why were the poor living in the lower town?

He went to his father's office and sat down in the armchair, frowning. 'I don't like it here anymore. Why are all those people here? They're disgusting.'

'I know, Davey. I know. They have to be here for the moment. There's nowhere else for them to go right now.'

'I hate them, Dad. I hate them. They stink and they're dirty. Can't you make them go away?'

'Don't worry,' the mayor replied, coming round the side of the desk and placing his hand on his son's head. 'I'm working on it. Soon you won't be bothered by them, okay?'

'But when, Dad? When?'

'Please David, I'm working now. We'll talk about this later.'

The boy left his father's office and saw Willem engaged in painting the south wall of the building. He took up a position against a tree, shaded from the sun, and watched, observing the regular pauses as the man swatted away flies that landed on his face to drink the sweat that formed there.

The Founding of Soutbek

The party set off in search of the river where months previously they had witnessed the herd of elephants. Due to !Urisis' pregnancy they travelled slowly, but their progress was steady. Van Meerman noticed that sometimes they would pass areas where stones and branches had been stacked. At these !Urisis and !Guŋbee would always pause and make a few additions to the piles. Asked the reason for this behaviour, !Urisis explained that the piles represented the graves of their ancestors or were cairns to the Namaqua god, Tsui-//goab, who often manifested himself in the form of a praying mantis. By laying down stones or branches she was honouring them. Fournier and Rootkop scoffed at her, asking what could a god who was nothing but an insect do? She told them that they misunderstood, but said no more.

A few days later the travellers found themselves without water, and with no clear idea of where they were. Van Meerman was certain that they should have reached the river two days previously. Anxiety was rife among the men, for they were frail without water and feared the hyenas which preyed on the weak. !Guŋbee tried to calm the men, explaining '*Tsui-//goab gum ni huidao*' (Tsui-//goab will help us). But van Meerman, frustrated and exhausted, began to lose faith in !Guŋbee. In a fury he turned to the man and shouted, 'I don't want to hear about your god again! I am sick of all these rituals, all this time wasted on an insect! You will never speak of him again!'

Yet, the next day !Guŋbee led the party, which had begun to lose hope, to the river of the elephants. After they had drunk their fill, !Guŋbee turned to van Meerman and said, '*Ti /hũtse //arits ke ko !gamte-ǂgao hã, χaveb ke Tsũi//goaba ko ǂkhātsi, tsĩ //eĩb ko nesiri hui !kheisa mũ-!ants ko //nai*' (Yesterday you could almost have killed me but Tsui-//goab refused to let you do so. Have you now convinced yourself that he has helped us?). Van Meerman did not record his reply.

In fact, very little of this portion of the journal is extant. The worst of the damage has occurred to these final pages, so that in some places two or three sheets at a time are unreadable. It seems that it took the travellers some time before they reached the mouth of the Oliphants River, and arrived here at this spot, where the river dried up in the 1920s, and where we now find the town of Soutbek.

Originally the intention was to make camp only for a few days in order to rest, before continuing in the direction Akembie had advised them to take. Unfortunately, the very next day storm clouds came in over the cliffs and the sea, and by afternoon the party were experiencing their first West Coast storm. Heavy rains, fierce winds and giant waves raged all around them. They huddled in their portable huts, rarely able to make forages into the surrounding region in order to gather what food they could find. Taking what was immediately visible, they lived on mussels and succulents for days.

After leaving the Namaqua *kraal*, !Guŋbee and !Urisis had shown the men how to make '*matjieshuisen*' (mat-houses). These were semi-permanent structures comprising a dome-shaped framework of saplings bound together with plant fibre. !Urisis had laboured long and hard to make enough sedge mats with which to cover each of the *matjieshuisen*. While these structures had been adequate shelter in the interior, they proved utterly useless in the violent coastal weather. Usually moisture would cause the sedge to expand and thus to become waterproof, but the rain that fell destroyed the mats completely. Within a few days no shelter remained to them. Concerned for his wife, and realising that they could not survive under such conditions, van Meerman began to search for other shelter. By great fortune he discovered a cave in the cliff-face along the shoreline of the bay. It was dry and offered protection from the cold. The party moved in immediately.

Evidently during this period the explorers' search for the gold was neglected; their primary focus became their own survival. It was a dreadful time. Freezing temperatures and little nourishment led to the members of the party falling into despair one by one. Squabbles broke out among the men and one night Heller attacked !Guŋbee, saying that the '*vuile Hottentoo*' (dirty Hottentot) had purposely led them there to die.

Believing themselves to be waiting only for death, the party continued weakening each day. However, part way through the winter, what van Meerman describes as a '*mirakel*' (miracle) occurred. A band of *strandlopers* (their specific tribal name is not recorded) came to the cave. It was a regular dwelling place of theirs and they were surprised to find inside it five white men, one Namaqua male and a pregnant Namaqua woman. At first they reacted with hostility, for among the tribes of South Africa it had for centuries been understood that each band had a territory of its own, marked by a specific watering hole. To hunt or live within that territory without permission was to incite war. But before any harm could be done, !Urisis stepped forward and spoke to the band of *strandlopers*, explaining their situation. They had only to look at the heavily pregnant woman and the bedraggled men to change from hostile to sympathetic. They agreed to make peace with the interlopers and to share the cave with them.

It was thanks to the intervention of the *strandlopers* that the explorers did not die during that first winter; for the *strandlopers* showed them how to gather food, pointing out which roots and berries were edible, and where the best water was to be found. /Khunibeb, the chief of the small tribe, apologised to van Meerman through the *tolcq* !Guŋbee about being so protective over their land. He explained that in their culture the territory of each tribal band was handed down from father to son. This meant that each band developed a strong bond with the landscape, a bond which was reinforced by stories relating to particular features within that landscape. /Khunibeb explained further that the small tribe of which he was chief had only been living in the area for five generations, as they had been ousted from their previous territory by a rival tribe. The loss of their territory had been difficult to come to terms with and they were only just beginning to form a strong bond with their new landscape. /Khunibeb leaned forward and told van Meerman, 'Do you see? For our people to lose their land means to lose everything.' The chief's words obviously touched van Meerman, for in the manuscript they are underlined twice. And in a later entry he observes, '*Wij beginnen ook nu deel van het land te worden*' (We, too, are becoming part of the land).

As her pregnancy progressed, van Meerman records that !Urisis became increasingly concerned about having her baby away from her family and their traditions. But the old women of /Khunibeb's tribe, sensing her fears, stepped in and cared for her. Though their rituals were different to those she had learnt from her own people, they seemed to comfort the girl. And when finally, the pains of labour came to her, she let the old women send van Meerman out of the hut in order to make a small fire which he was to keep going throughout the birth process. No pots were to be put on the fire, nor was anything allowed to be cooked or roasted on it. The old women warned that both mother and child would go blind if this practice was neglected. Van Meerman records that only once the newborn's screams were heard was he allowed to enter the cave again. There he watched as the umbilical cord was cut with a knife and the bleeding staunched with a plaster of mud. The baby was not allowed to be washed with water, and was only cursorily wiped with some grass, before being wrapped in a kaross and placed in !Urisis' arms. They named their newborn son Pieter !Urisibgeiste van Meerman.

By the time spring came, both Perreira and Rootkop had met women of their own from the *strandloper* band and were happily in love. Flowers began blooming in the *veld* all around the area. The mass blossoming, the abundance of colour and the quiet beauty of the area, as well as newfound romance, made the explorers forget about their expedition and the gold. Soon Perreira's wife was pregnant, and the men began building houses of stone on the hill so that there would be permanent shelter to protect them in both summer and winter.

Together, the *strandloper* men and van Meerman's troop constructed low stone barriers in the intertidal zones of the rocky bay. Waves swept fish in, and the fish, unable to escape, were easily caught. To this day the remains of these stone walls are visible at low tide in the bays of Soutbek. In fact, many of the original stones were used in the building of the fish factory in the late 1960s. The factory still stands, and on any day one can see a number of colourful boats on the water. It is a comfort to know that though centuries have passed, the inhabitants of Soutbek are still as reliant on fishing as their forefathers were.

It is after these events that van Meerman's journal tapers off. Life beside the sea with his son, wife and others seems to have taken up the bulk of his energy, with little time to spare for keeping a journal. Other than some minor entries about catching fish and the growth of his son, nothing further is reported. However, it is evident that the diverse group lived peacefully amongst the *strandloper* band. Many children were born, and many friendships were made. Life at the mouth of the river was idyllic.

From the official records of the Compagnie we can determine that van Meerman and his small tribe did their best not to be detected, for when the Compagnie sent the ship *Bruijdegom* in August of 1667 to determine '*off de Oliphantsreviers aldaer niet in zee ujtloopt*' (whether the Oliphants River flows into the sea there), they found only the river, which they established was too shallow for transport. They saw no signs of human life and reported back to the Commander that the West Coast was too violent and dangerous for habitation. In 1669 another ship, *Grundel*, was sent to explore the West Coast. Their report confirmed that that area of the continent was '*dood*' (dead) and economically utterly unrewarding. It was many years before any further exploration of this area was carried out.

The result of the Compagnie's neglect of the West Coast meant that van Meerman and his tribe of followers were able to establish for themselves a town based on communal living, sharing and acceptance. Therefore, while their expedition had begun as a quest for gold, for van Meerman and his party of explorers there was in the end no great wealth, no rich city of gold, but what they found was worth more than any treasure could ever be.

Late afternoon, the mayor allowed the boy to sit in the driver's seat of his car. He showed him how the clutch and gears worked, letting him drive unsteadily up the hill, before helping him with the handbrake when he parked at the end of the tar road. The boy unclasped his seatbelt and got out of the car to wait for his dad to turn it around before he drove back. But, after getting out himself, the mayor removed the key from the ignition and locked the doors.

'What now?' David asked.

'I want to show you something.'

'I thought you were showing me how to drive.'

'I am. I am. There's time for all that. This won't take long.'

Together they walked the short distance to where the shacks of the upper town began. As they walked through the streets the inhabitants waved, others came up and shook hands with man and boy.

'Mr Mayor,' they said, 'see how we're living now.'

'I see, yes. Don't you worry, though. I am fixing it. You know you can rely on me.'

'We know, Mr Mayor, and we're so thankful. God bless you, sir.'

'You see that?' the mayor said to the boy. 'You see how they love me, how they depend on me?'

They had stopped at a plot of land cornered by bricks and weeds, a makeshift shack in the middle. A dog lay in the sand before the shack, wagging its tail at them and whining quietly.

'That is what you must remember, David. I am burdened by them. Long ago, back in 1993, they said everything was going to change. Men came in their BMWs, black men, white men, they threw T-shirts at the people. They made speeches and promises. And then they drove away and forgot about us. So it became my burden, you see.'

'Can we go now? Are you finished?'

The mayor looked around at the shacks, the abandoned plots, the dirt in the streets.

'This is the street I grew up in.' He pointed to some rubble lying nearby. 'I can't even tell you whether those bricks come from my house or not. It's nothing now, my house. I couldn't find it if I tried.'

'Dad, *come on*, I want to leave now.'

'Listen to me, Davey, listen to what I'm telling you: this will not be your burden. I am doing all I can so that you will not inherit this.'

No longer did Willem meet with the women in the evenings. He was unwelcome since the boy's return and with the mayor's regular presence. He read on his own, well into the night, before walking down the hill to sleep beside Sara, leaving again at dawn. Three times he had read *The History*, attracted by the utopia it described. He was drawn ever closer to the past, to its answers for a better life. He knew that Oom Bekkie was the oldest man in the village and he went to find him, preparing questions to put to him about Soutbek and its history.

The old man had regularly strolled in the fields or walked long distances on the beach, searching for things he put no name to. But on this day as so often now, he sat near the sloop, a hat on his head, wearing a shirt, tie and jacket with sweat stains under the arms, as though uneasy on land, a guest.

'A warm day today, Oom Bekkie.'

'On land yes, but that water, see the way the waves ripple over there?' he pointed, 'like ice. When it's calm like that with that silver ripple and a grey colour even if the sky is blue, then you know.'

'You've lived here a long time, *Oom*.'

'My whole life, never been anywhere else, never will.'

'What do you remember about this place when you were young?'

'The fish. There were so many fish back then. I remember the shoals and shoals my dad and older brother brought in just by themselves. That was before the fish factory you know, 1942. I worked there from the day it opened. In 1963 our weight was a million and a half tons.'

'But what else? What about the town?'

'Ah, 1976. That was another big year. But you won't remember that. Water was like tea it was so warm.'

'But *Oom*, the people? How did they live? Can you remember? What about the lower town? And where did the people come from?'

'Let me tell you what I was told by my grandmother. And what I told the mayor too when he came asking a few years ago.'

'He asked you?'

'For that book, I suppose. Must have wanted to know, same as you. Though it doesn't seem he put anything about that in it. I haven't read it you know, but I heard about it and it doesn't seem he put the history in there.'

'What history?'

'The people. You know these big storms we have here – there was that one just the other day. Well, this was a massive storm. Washed up a creature on the shore, half man half fish. A woman living in that cave – you know the one at the white cliffs, at the bend – she found him and nursed him back to health, fell in love with him and bore him children. But he missed the ocean and he left. The children became the people of Soutbek, half fish, salt water in their veins and that's why we go to sea, looking for our daddy. We want to catch him, bring him home. We miss him.'

'But where did this woman come from, *Oom*?'

'I never found him myself, and I'm too old now to go searching, but I hear his voice on the waves, calling me to him.' The man looked out at the sea, his eyes milky, small in the glare off the waves.

'But isn't there anything more, *Oom*? Anything real?'

The man coughed a bit, leaning heavily on his walking stick. 'You know why they call me Oom Bekkie?'

'It's not your name?'

'It started as Oom Soutbek, because of living here so long, and then it got shorter and shorter to Bekkie – *little mouth*. That's me now, little mouth, no one wants to hear what I have to say.'

Willem wanted other accounts of the past, but there was no library, and few people in the town owned such books. There was only one person he could think of who might have any of interest. Yet he detested the man, a man so unnatural, so removed from the company of others, nor could he forget his previous political affiliations. Still, Willem's need was greater than his dislike of the professor and he chose to approach him.

Weeds, three, four feet high grew in front of the professor's house. The walls were stained, the windows filthy. Willem flattened a path for himself through the undergrowth to the front door. There was no response to his knock. He waited and knocked again. Through the glass of the door he could make out a shadow moving into the hallway. He knocked again. The shadow came forward, and spoke without opening the door. 'I don't want a gardener.'

'No, that's not why I came, sir.'

'I don't have any money.'

'No, it's not that. I came because of the book. I read it, the one you wrote with the mayor.'

'What about it?' the professor asked, partly opening the door.

'I was wondering, are there others? I mean, have you written others? It says so on the inside cover.'

'If it says so then why are you bothering to ask?' the professor snapped, taking a step back into the dark hallway.

Willem flushed. He had planned his words carefully in advance, forgetting them now.

'Please,' he said. 'I was wondering, I know it's a lot to ask, but I'm so interested and there's nowhere else. Please. Can I read them?'

'You can do whatever the hell you want, I don't care!' He began to close the door.

'Wait!' Willem called, reaching out to grab at the handle. 'Please! I meant can I borrow them? Can I borrow your books from you?'

The professor opened the door again, peering out at the boy standing, waiting. He recognised him now. 'You're the mayor's nephew, aren't you?'

'That's right.'

For some time he remained as he was, leaning against the open door, glaring at the boy.

'Well, come in, if you must. Just don't touch anything.'

It had been many years since the professor had had a visitor. The filth on the windows and the high weeds kept the house dark. Though it was early afternoon he had lamps on in all of the rooms. A dreadful odour filled the house; rotting apple cores and brimming ashtrays. A full litter box stood beside an armchair in the lounge. Cats, two of them, though perhaps there were more, slept on paper stacks. Books covered the couches, tables and chairs; everywhere was paper, blank or scribbled on in illegible handwriting. The professor moved aside some of these papers, and selected a red hardback from the floor.

'One at a time,' he said, handing it across for Willem to take. 'You won't get another one until I get this one back. Do you hear me? In the same condition. No candle wax, no stains, no pen marks.'

'Yes, sir. Of course.'

An Overview of Native Tribes of Southern Africa before 1652 by T.W. Pearson was dated 1974 and contained no illustrations other than a few maps. Willem began reading it that night as Sara slept, deliberate in his progress, so that within two days he was able to return it and borrow another. No requests were permitted; he took them in the order that they came, reading everything with the same interest. Continuing in this fashion, he worked his way through the books written by the professor and was soon reading works by other authors which had been used as references in the man's research. For Willem patterns began to emerge. He came to believe that history was not about dates and people. It was about mastery: the mastery of others and the mastery of land. It began with the tribes who fought one another for livestock, for grazing land, for the bodies of their ancestors which had been forged into mountains and streams, making the landscape strangely human, a cairn to the living and the dead. Then the Europeans came, different groups of them, who fought amongst themselves and against the tribes, fighting for ownership of the Cape and its interior. Through his reading Willem began to see the past as a machine. It ate people as it went, ingesting the land, leaving nothing for the weak, the poor. This vision amplified for Willem the futility of painting the wall. What was its purpose? To improve a town in which he was unwelcome, in which he owned nothing? For twenty years he had lived on the cliff tops, accepting the fact of his poverty, the poverty of his neighbours. But since reading about Pieter van Meerman's wish for independence and a place of his own, Willem began to feel that Soutbek was as much his as the mayor's.

'I won't do it anymore!' he told himself. He would no longer accept the mayor's money. He would build a house for his family. He would no longer allow himself to be mastered.

'I won't paint that wall one more time!' he repeated, but they were only words. He could not afford to put any meaning behind them.

After receiving confirmation of his plan, the mayor called a meeting for all inhabitants of the upper town. With the town hall still occupied by squatting families, they assembled instead on the Mayor's Wife's Beach. The mayor stood on the porch of the store, his wife and son on either side of him. Anna wore a new dress, make-up and jewellery for the occasion. She was prettier than usual that day, feeling proud as she waited for the crowd to settle.

For David, too, the anticipation was immense. He had heard his father's speeches before and looked up to this man whose voice could carry across hundreds of people and be heard over the sound of the waves. He looked out at the faces that were turned up towards his father. They were the faces of hardship, of homelessness and despair, as though beaten and left for dead. Even in the children's faces there remained nothing smooth or clear. He had seen vagrants, smelled them in the town where he went to boarding school and also in Genot. He had seen that they were all the same, the faces of the neglected; there was no means of distinguishing one from the next; each shared with the others the same texture, the same shrivelled appearance. Here, before him, the thronging bodies on the beach had been reduced to a single mass of bones and flesh. That mass took on the shape of a large body with a single face, a face with a wide open mouth, above a body with two hands outstretched, wanting.

The mayor cleared his throat in preparation. He was excited. He had had an idea of dignity and that idea was about to be fulfilled. He would eliminate the reminders of his early life – degradation, humiliation; that misery which had followed him wherever he went, touching all he owned and did. He cleared his throat again and raised his hand for silence.

'Thank you to everyone for coming today. I know these past few months have been difficult and I want to thank you for handling the situation so well. I wish that there was more I could have done, but these things take time. As you know, there is always so much red tape to be got through. However, I have not forgotten you or your situation: I have been making demands on your behalf and finally the time has come when your faith in me and your patience will be rewarded. Things are about to change for you. I have made arrangements for improving your lives. Within the next few months each family from the upper town will receive a new home made from proper bricks and cement. The houses will come with electricity and running water and a bathroom. You will no longer have to sleep on the sand. Your children will have roofs over their heads.'

On the beach a wave of chatter rose. Some began to cheer. Others were speechless, hugging their husbands, their neighbours. They whispered to each other and words could not come to them fast enough. The noise of the crowd stirred nearby seagulls, which flew up over their heads, across the houses of the lower town and past the cliffs of the upper town. Questions began to be called out.

'When? When will the houses be built?'

'How much will it cost?'

'How big will they be?'

The mayor motioned again for silence. 'You must not worry. It will cost you nothing. You will not be expected to pay for anything other than the water and electricity you use once you have moved in. Now, please, please,' he called as other questions came from the crowd. 'Please be patient. This is simply a preliminary meeting to inform you of what the future holds for you. In the next week I and my associates will meet personally with each family and discuss their individual needs.'

He lowered his arms and bowed to the crowd. Then taking his wife and son by their hands, he went home.

After his speech, the inhabitants of the upper town stood in clusters, talking.

'But will they pull down our houses?' one of them asked another. 'My grandfather built our house. My father was born in it. I was born in it. My children were born in it.'

'Yes,' replied another, 'and where are you living now? What's the good of having a pile of rubbish if it can't protect your family from the wind and rain?'

Others nodded at this wisdom, murmuring assent.

'A house built by a stranger is better than a crumbling brick laid by your grandfather,' they said.

Soon however, the same people began to recall the housing promised to them by the Reconstruction and Development Programme a decade or more before. Despite the allocation it had been more than three years before building had begun.

'Three years?' the younger inhabitants asked.

'Oh yes,' the older ones replied, listing in unison the reasons they had been given for the delay: shortage of water, theft of materials, problems with sewage disposal, and mostly, shortage of funds. In the end only twenty houses had been built, most of which had been destroyed by a fire shortly afterwards.

'We know, you see,' the older people said, 'not to hold our breaths. Perhaps the houses will come, or perhaps not, but autumn is hard on our heels. You will find us frozen to death on the packing floors of the fish factory before a single brick is laid.'

At this the crowd stood silent. Almost as one they looked out at the grey sea behind them, the dull sky above. They felt no words inside them. They felt only a sharp recognition of what it was to have days and months pass without pause, without any pause; recognition of what it was to be led towards hope and then denied. The broken margins of the Mayor's Wife's Beach formed a border around the silent crowd. They could see nothing of the upper town from where they stood. Removed as they were from it, at this distance so small, they found themselves unable to imagine it as anything other than what it was. They could not picture it in any previous condition nor could they imagine what it might look like if rebuilt.

A child began to cry, and at that sound the mothers on the beach returned to themselves, saw their family members around them beginning to shiver in the cooling air. Calling their children, they turned back towards the hill, walking unsteadily along the dirt path which ran through the dry riverbed, returning to the upper town and to what homes they had.

Yet within a few days a difference in the upper towners was already noticeable. A difference in the way they walked, in the words they chose when speaking to each other, to their masters and mistresses in the lower town. They walked more upright, spoke more clearly. Something akin to pride had been returned to them, for they bore now a hope of shelter, and, though the word was not common to them, they felt themselves moving towards civilisation. They would be people again.

Willem remained on the beach after everyone else had left. He had heard the mayor's announcement with neither joy nor grief. There was something inevitable about the news, as though all of his life had been moving in the direction of this obligation. Once the houses came, he knew, they would all, each member of the upper town, be beholden to the mayor, beholden without relief. They would be shackled to lifetime after lifetime of painting walls, of cleaning ever increasing numbers of unused rooms. He could not accept the house, he decided. And yet, his mother sat all day in a rank corner, pissing onto newspapers, while his sister sat beside her, growing old and ugly.

From the sea a mist began to roll in. It shifted across the small bay, covering the streets and houses. The town quivered, vanishing swiftly, but through the mist he could still make out the south-facing wall of the town hall. Where everything else was shaded by fog, the wall stood out, as though all things dark had formed a rim around it. With the mist the air had turned cold, and Willem, suddenly shivering, turned up the collar of his work-jacket, put his hands into his pockets. A lone seagull returned from the cliffs and perched itself on a rock nearby, silent, eyes closed against the cool air. He thought again of the promised houses. There was no rejecting such an offer; even without the house he was indebted to the mayor. Even without the house he would spend the rest of his life working off the debt of his family's poverty.

Along the coastline the weather remained warm. Here and there midges began to appear, until within a week clouds of them hovered in doorways and near trees. They flew around people's eyes and mouths, looking for moisture to settle on. The threat of autumn was forgotten as the inhabitants of Soutbek walked with waving arms and squinting eyes, their lips tightly shut against the insects.

Willem led Sara through the upper town towards the plot on which his father's house had stood. Despite the lapse of time and the green shrubs which had grown over the rubble, there remained still a smell of cinders, a smell of things not quite gone. He showed her the litter of glass and charred brick. 'We will live here. I will tell the mayor that our house must be built right on this spot.'

He pointed to the left and right, at other patches of rubble, mentioning those who had lived there before; people who would return, who would be their neighbours. People she knew neither by face nor by name.

'They will help us,' he said, 'and we will help them. When you need some sugar or milk, when the children need watching.'

Walking through the streets of the upper town with Willem, Sara recognised little from her first visit. In the intervening months shrubs and small orange flowers had grown, and the streets were less empty, the smell less acrid. It was not until they approached the church and the cemetery that Sara remembered anything clearly. The same well-trodden earth remained; the same dusty plant grew from the low bell tower. In the cemetery, too, nothing seemed altered. Only the three graves of those buried on the day she arrived were different now; indistinguishable from the rest.

'This is where we buried my father,' Willem said, pointing at a grave towards the centre of the cemetery. A pile of soil, covered by a fishing net placed over a wooden frame, marked the position of the body. In places the net was broken and the same green and orange weeds Sara had seen throughout the town grew up through these holes. At the head of the grave stood the upright from a wooden cross; bleached, rotting. No crosspiece remained, and so there was no name, no dates to show his life and death.

For Willem's brother, Paul, there was no marker at all. Willem was able only to point vaguely towards a spot, overrun with weeds.

'We had no money, then,' Willem said, an apology.

They walked a little way, treading carefully. Willem reached over and took her hand.

'This is where I saw you for the first time,' he said.

'Yes,' she said, and his hand in hers was cold, the hand of a corpse.

When Willem had first come to Sara, knocking at the door late at night, she was aware of what he wanted. Though sheltered as a child, she had learnt enough of the relations between men and women from her mother and the migrant workers who had come to their house from time to time in search of food and shelter. Seeing Willem standing before her, his eyes downcast, his cheeks pale, Sara had recalled those homeless men who stood on the doorstep, pointing at their tired feet, their empty bellies, the lowering sun.

They came from the north mostly, the migrants, from the gold mines. Their stories were all the same: the mines were closing. Nothing remained to dig for. There were no more jobs. The land had been used up. So they had come south, having heard that a vast tract of cultivated land followed a large river, a river which led towards the sea. No one starved in the South they said, because there was so much; farmers gave away fruit, the sea was full of fish and other things to eat. Any man could live there and have enough to feed even the largest family. In the South there was plenty. They spoke of the sea as though they had been away for a long time and were now returning, as though they had known it themselves; but their knowledge was formed entirely from rumour. They did not know it at all.

Sara brought out her picture of the sea and asked them, 'Is this what it looks like?'

'Yes,' they replied, their voices trembling, eyes bright at the first sight of their futures. 'That is the sea. That is where we will live.'

Having no reason to disbelieve them, Sara began to feel that she too knew the sea.

After dinner, she would make up a bed for the travellers on the floor; a sleeping bag, a pillow, an extra blanket if it was cold. But more often than not she found the bedding untouched the following morning, and understood what the rhythmic creaking from her mother's room had meant. She did not blame her mother for this; she too was coming to terms with solitude and with her own changing body. She too wished for the warmth of someone next to her, for the touch of a hand on her skin.

Standing in the cemetery beside the graves, Sara pointed up towards the sky, which was turning pink and orange. She held Willem's hand, pressing it against her.

'Look,' she said, 'isn't it beautiful?'

'Yes,' he replied.

'And what makes it even more wonderful,' she continued, 'is knowing that your father and brother would have seen the same thing, and even before that, all those hundreds of years ago, your ancestors would have shared this view when they started the town.'

'There were people here long before that,' Willem answered. He turned away from the view. The church was darkening in the twilight. Soon it would be night.

'I know,' Sara replied, 'but this is different. We're talking about you being descended from adventurers and pioneers. Doesn't that make you feel proud?'

He removed his hand from hers. 'No, we're not the children of pioneers. We're the children of slaves.'

'What do you mean?'

Willem gestured, taking in the landscape. 'The people in this area have always had someone telling them what to do.

First by tribal warring, they were bullied into this corner. Then the explorers came and took this land from them and made them take care of them, and then more people came and took the land from them. There is always someone that is stronger.'

Sara shook her head, 'But that's not what happened. It wasn't like that.'

'How do you know? Were you here?'

'No, of course not, but *The History* says...'

Willem interrupted, moving away from her, 'History says that for centuries humans have been trying to rule other humans, taking the land and everything else for themselves. That's all the history you need to know. There is nothing else.'

In Anna the aftermath of the mayor's speech had been immense. Already the absence of affection for her husband had waned in the weeks since first reading *The History*. Now, even more so, she felt that she had been cruel, that she had not understood him. In all those years she had believed him to be a monster, he had been making this life. A life in which he gave homes to the poor, in which he helped others without show. All that she had begun to suspect about him had been proven. He was god-like, colossal. As a child begging forgiveness, she turned towards him. In bed she breathed his exhalations, pressing her body against his. Each of his arrivals home in the evening she greeted with warmth and touch.

More than anything else, she forgave the boy his parentage, no longer seeing in him the horror of rotting flesh she had before. She began by tidying his room, feeling a fondness for the clothes she picked up, the bed she made. With the help of Sara, biscuits in the shape of cricket bats followed, and in the afternoon the two women sought him out for card games on the patio. In some ways she still feared the boy, but he was becoming a son, something he had not been before. In her new role as mother she began to think of her family; her parents, her siblings. Perhaps she could search for them now, bring them to Soutbek? They could live in the upper town. Surely Pieter would organise homes for them along with all the others? Surely there would be space for them now? After all, how many empty rooms did they not have? Half-asleep she turned her imagining into fact, making children out of adults. Her siblings played on her beach, shared her house, causing all the rooms to come alive with sound.

'It's so wonderful what you are doing,' she murmured, touching Pieter's side.

'I told you,' he said, softly, placing his papers on the bedside table and leaning towards her, so that the bones of her shoulders pushed against his arm. She was so small. He wanted to fill in the fragile parts of her. 'I told you I would take care of you and give you a better life.'

'I know,' she replied, resting her head against him. 'But this isn't for me. This is for everyone else, and that's what makes it so wonderful.'

'But it's for you mostly,' he said, kissing her brow. He tilted her chin towards his mouth and brought his lips to hers. Both had forgotten what it was to be kissed. For Anna every place he kissed, every place he touched, felt as though it belonged to two people: the wife she had been for more than a decade, and a seventeen-year-old girl. This time there was nothing loathsome or fearful about it. His hands on her body were gentle. She could feel herself crawling into those hands, guiding them. In their lovemaking there was nothing like pain or degradation. He became for her something sacred, and for him, the free entry into her body, the ready access to what he had yearned for, was as much as to return to their first kiss beside the tortoise in the field, and to begin again.

Afterwards she lay with her head on his chest, with her hand on the rise and fall of his belly. Light from the passage lay on the open cupboard door, lighting the bottles of lotion, pots of cream, perfumes and clothes.

Beside her Pieter spoke, 'I was right, wasn't I? Good things come to those who wait.'

'Yes, you were right.'

'And once they're gone you will see all the good that will come of it.'

'Once who are gone?'

'The upper towners, of course. You don't think I am going to let them stay do you?'

Anna sat up, her cheek cooling where it had moved away from his skin. 'What are you saying?' she asked. 'What about the houses? You promised them houses.'

'Yes, and they will get them. A spot has been selected, about ten kilometres down the coast. They'll still be by the sea. Nothing will change for them. It will be better actually.'

Naked, she rose from the bed. Her nightgown lay on the floor on his side of the bed. She picked up her pillow and held it in front of her body. 'How?' she asked. 'How will it be better? These are their homes.'

'Homes? They don't even have homes. I am giving them homes.'

'But this is where they live.'

'And what way of life is it? I am helping them.'

He leaned his head back on the pillow, reaching his hand out to her, 'Come, lie down again. Don't worry about this, it's not anything for you to worry about. It will be fine.'

She trembled, her right hand brushing over her hair. She walked around to the side of the bed and reached down to pick up her nightdress, all the while holding the pillow in front of her. 'What you are doing is wrong. You cannot remove people from their homes.'

'I don't see what the problem is. I'm rescuing them,' he replied.

'And *The History*?'

'What about it?'

'The history of this area is the history of these people. It's not the history of retired farmers and professors.'

'You forget that I am from the upper town. It's my history too. I want to make something of this town and that can't happen if it stays like this. It means moving people to better conditions, it means making changes.'

She was begging now, kneeling in front of him. 'No, no, no, you can't do it. It isn't right. It's a massacre.'

Surely he couldn't be this. He couldn't only be this. 'All that time you spent compiling and researching. I thought you believed in the past of Soutbek. I thought you believed in its lessons about everyone living together. You wrote it down. *The History* ...'

The mayor threw the sheet from him and shouted, '*The History*! *The History*! Shut up about the fucking *History*! *The History* is a lie!'

'What?'

'A lie. I made it up. Every single part of it was made up by me and Terence.'

Anna stared at him, on her knees still. 'I don't understand.'

'It doesn't exist. There is no *History*. I am *The History*.'

He watched the woman rising slowly from the floor and moving away from him, watching still as she walked towards the cupboard. He could see her back, her narrow thighs. There was so little to her, as though she had been cut from cardboard.

'What are you doing?' he asked as she began to dress.

She spoke with difficulty, hearing her voice falter at first, 'I – I – I don't want to be here anymore.'

Only then did she run, escaping through the doorway into the empty passages of the house. In the dark she could see nothing, walls and empty space looked the same. She moved as though blind, feeling her way by memory. From the bedroom sounds came of her husband dressing, and she knew he would come after her. She knew he would follow her and that she had to get out of the house before he could find her. She had not realised that she was screaming, until suddenly her hand fell on something warm, something alive, and she stopped.

'Ma?' it said, 'What's wrong?'

Anna felt the warm circle of flesh in her hand; it was the child, the boy. Underneath her fingers she could feel his skin. It was monstrous. She heard the voice of her husband in the dark, and pushed the child from her, running outside.

Anna woke late. She had slept enough, was not cold or hungry. The room she woke in was bare. Its windows were covered in newspaper, the floor hard beneath her. She smelled ash, urine. In slow detail the previous night returned to her. She remembered the taste of him, his declarations. The bathroom door had been open, its light on. The bedroom door too, despite the boy. A view of themselves reflected back to her in the bathroom mirror. The gaping mouth of the bedroom door. The house had been breathing heavily, its walls damp and warm as skin. Grey they were, and white, each in its own state of completion, casting shadows. A boundless copulation of room embracing room, of passages entering one another, of room opening up on room, a warm embrace, many-armed.

Beside her Sara stirred and Anna shifted uncomfortably, giving her more room. Again she dozed, half-dreaming the conversation being held in low tones in the corner of the room.

A young woman's voice: 'What do you think he will do when he finds that girl has brought his wife here? When he finds that you've taken them in?'

There was no response.

'He will stop the money. What will we do then, what about Ma?'

It was some time before Willem replied, 'She's left him, Trudie. How can we leave her to live outside?'

'Let her go to the town hall then,' she hissed. 'Let her eat at the soup kitchen like everyone else.'

'You can't mean that.'

'I don't understand why you're bothering with her. She's nothing to us.'

But in the mid-morning it was Trudie who joined the queue at the soup kitchen, bringing back food to share with the women.

'It's only for today. Tomorrow they can look after themselves,' she told her brother.

They ate in silence, and afterwards, without announcement, Anna spoke. There was no haste in her retelling of what had passed between herself and the mayor. Her features unmoving, her hands folded, she told about the plan to remove the people of the upper town. 'There will be houses, but the upper town will be gone. Everyone will be moved,' she explained.

'He hates it so much that it's not enough for him not to live in it anymore,' Willem said. 'He has to remove it completely.'

'He lied about *The History* too,' she continued, telling what she knew.

Willem sickened at the news. The pages he had read, what had they been? What did it make of him? 'What *is* the history of this place then?' he asked.

'The same as it was before the book,' Sara said. 'Nothing has changed really.'

'No, that's not true. We can't pretend that it hasn't changed anything.'

He was vengeful, sick with it. Leaving the house, he told no one where he was going, taking coins for the pay phone when his sister's back was turned.

A small group had gathered, some three or four neighbours, curious as to the presence of the mayor's wife. On his return Willem drank from a quart of beer he was offered, cleared the dust from his throat before observing, 'Tomorrow or the next day there will be a newspaper headline of interest to you.' He then proceeded to tell the story as he had heard it from Anna. Each person present carried it away with them, passing it on to others. Despite hearing it a number of times removed from the original, Oom Bekkie was the one who crystallised the format, adding a rhythm to the sentences and words, so that they sounded like wisdom. With the result that, though they had heard it before, the inhabitants sought him out to hear it from him time and time again.

'I've lived here my whole life. I knew that history wasn't mine. I come from the sea,' he said.

But many did not believe what they heard. They could not accept it as true. If the mayor's wife wanted to leave him so be it, but leave it at that, there was no need for the rest.

David had been pushed against a wall, had cut his forehead. His father picked him up, half-dressed, shoeless. He held a cloth against the blood, pressing hard to make it stop.

'She pushed me, just pushed me out of the way like I was attacking her or something.'

'Listen,' the mayor said, 'it was an accident. Your mother is very sorry.'

'If she's sorry then where is she? Where was she running to?'

'She had a little fright, that's all. She'll be back soon. I was going to go after her, but we can wait for her to come back, can't we, while we sort out your head?'

'What's wrong with her?'

His father dropped the cloth in the sink. 'She's upset because I'm trying to fix the town. She doesn't understand that I am doing this for you – you will inherit this. It will be yours.'

'What are you talking about? Mayors don't have heirs, Dad.'

He smiled. 'But I will make it better and when you are older you will come here and there will be no burden.'

'Jesus, Dad, do you want to know what the real burden is? It's having to hear you go on and on about this fucking place. Just on and on and on. If it's such a burden then why don't you leave it? Why make us stay here and suffer in this shit hole?'

'But it's for you, Davey. I...'

The boy stood up from where he had been perching on the side of the bath. 'I keep telling you that I don't want it. This place means nothing to me. I don't want it. Just forget about it now. I've had enough of fucking Soutbek!'

The next day David arranged to join a friend at his parents' holiday home for the last week of the vacation. The mayor drove him, placing in his hand a number of notes. 'Let me know when it runs out, okay? And you phone me when you need me. Just phone and I will come fetch you.'

It was dark when he returned, the house dark too. He walked from room to room, switching on lights. She had not come back. In the bathroom he opened the cabinet and tidied all of her things. He straightened a towel, wiped out the basin. Next he went to the outside room. It was unlocked, the bed unmade. The girl was gone too. He sat down on the bed; it was cool, smelling of bodies and sleep. He put his face to the pillow; it was not her smell, but it was human.

She would return, he knew. The next day surely; where could two girls go without money? He would not be home when she returned. He would not let her see him waiting. In the morning he walked down to his office, humming quietly. She would be back by the time he returned. She would have tidied the kitchen and made the beds. He would forgive her. All would be well. He turned towards his office, noticing the wall of the town hall. It was white again. It had not been painted for a few days. 'Where's that idiot boy?' He had become annoying recently. Always hanging around the girl. Always coming to speak to his wife. The mayor paused, feeling a fool as he realised. 'That stupid boy!' he muttered to himself, and then louder, 'That stupid fucking boy!'

He would go up the hill. He would bring her back. He was the mayor for fuck's sake. He was the goddamn fucking mayor! Turning towards the upper town, the mayor noticed two ladies from the Women's Committee standing across the road staring at him and whispering.

He waved at them from where he stood, calling 'Nice morning, isn't it?'

They nodded and walked away.

'It can wait,' he thought. 'It can wait till later. I will go later.' For the second time that morning he changed direction, treading heavily towards the shop at the bottom of the steep hill.

The porch was empty, but from inside the mayor could hear the sound of many voices. As he stepped over the threshold, the rush of voices fell silent. Before him bodies of lower towners moved aside, clearing a path for him. There were no returns to his greetings. The mayor moved uneasily. Did they know about Anna?

In front of the counter, beside the dusty packets of biltong, he reached out for a paper – it was the last one, he saw. The headline caught his eye: *Forced Removals and Fake History.*

He read no further, registering hastily the newspapers in the hands of the assembled people. Not waiting for his change, saying nothing, the mayor rushed from the store, feeling the noise recommencing, rising like a wave behind him.

It was only once he reached his office that the mayor allowed himself to lay the paper out on the desk in front of him. He skimmed through, horrified by the phrases he read.

> Allegedly promised homes... ten kilometres away from the town... out of sight.
>
> Professor Terence Pearson, affiliated with pro-apartheid propaganda...
>
> Mayor of Soutbek, Pieter Fortuin, one-time fisherman...

Fisherman? Where had they got that from? He had never been a fisherman.

> Professor Hugh Priestly of... and Dr Harold Adonis... experts in the field, concur that there exist certain incongruities in dates and information... 'It could not be other than a fake,' Dr Adonis testifies.

The mayor groaned when he came to the final paragraph, which explained that despite the reporter's best efforts Mayor Fortuin was unreachable, and Professor Pearson had refused to comment when contacted.

He picked up the phone, feeling a rising sense of fury as he dialled, so that when eventually he heard the voice of the professor answering, he shouted, 'What is this? They phone you and you say nothing to me about it. You don't warn me. I have to find out in front of the whole town from a newspaper!'

'I thought it was a hoax,' the professor replied.

'A hoax?'

'It has happened to me many times during my professional career. It is what happens.'

'But they're saying it's a fake. How can they know that? You fucked up! It's your fault! They're saying it's full of dates that don't make sense. You're a professor of history! I thought history was all about dates! How could you get them wrong?'

'I didn't get them wrong. Not the real ones.'

'You're a fucking idiot!' the mayor shouted, slamming the phone down.

By the afternoon several reporters had phoned the mayor in his office. He side-stepped all questions, commenting on nothing, speaking without commitment, until finally he grew tired and unplugged the phone at the wall. Outside he could hear the buzz of the soup queue forming. He put his head in his hands, placing his elbows on his desk, dragging his palms over his cheeks. So much noise. Always so much noise from them. The hungry, the homeless; they sat on his shoulders, they hung round his neck.

As he sat brooding, he noticed that the sun was already far along its course. It was late afternoon. It was too late for the queue to be forming. Getting up, he left his office, walked round the side of the town hall and saw that there was no queue. Instead, inhabitants of both the upper and lower towns stood in large groups, talking. Reporters moved amongst them, herding them in front of a film crew and microphones.

Those from the lower town were reticent, unwilling to reply to the questions posed. They were pushed out of the way by upper towners, who shouted out that the allegations against the mayor were false.

'We watched him grow up,' they said.

'We knew his father.'

'We played together when we were children.'

They called him a good man. They spoke of him with admiration and respect, listing all that he had done for them.

'He wouldn't do anything bad like that. He is one of us.'

'He wouldn't make us move away. He knows what Soutbek means to us.'

When they saw the mayor appear from behind the town hall the members of the upper town began to cheer. The reporters turned from them, running towards the mayor, calling out questions, blocking his way.

'What do you have to say about the accusation that your history of Soutbek is false?'

The mayor pushed through the mass, grimly. 'Soutbek is a wonderful town with a marvellous history. You can't fake that.'

'What about the original manuscript? Where is that?'

'Will you make the van Meerman manuscript available in order to prove your book's authenticity?'

'It is in a private collection,' the mayor replied. 'It is not for me to say.'

'Is it true that you are forcing people to move away from Soutbek?'

The mayor had reached his house. He turned on the doorstep and shielded his eyes from the sun. 'I have no idea what you are talking about. I love Soutbek and its people. I grew up here.'

He reached into his pocket and brought out his keys, turning his back on further questions, trying to unlock the door without any signs of haste.

Within days further information was leaked to the press by anonymous individuals. Names of bribed officials in the alleged removal scheme were released, their photos filling the newspapers, the evening news. Across the country the media fuelled an irate outcry. Citizens were outraged. Had there not been enough of this sort of thing in the past? Forced removals; doctored histories? In the wake of the uproar, pending investigation, the officials were suspended and the promised houses, so urgently fought for by the mayor, were rescinded; the documentation was taken into custody, null and void.

In the upper town the inhabitants assembled around the one or two television sets which were still in the possession of a few. They stared, abashed, at footage of their destroyed homes, their shacks, hearing the interspersed voice-overs of their words of faith in the mayor. Artistically, the segment was powerful, with its careful use of juxtaposition to enhance the tragic irony of the situation. Yet for those watching on scratchy screens in the upper town, aesthetics meant very little. They understood only that they had been made fools of. That they had been turned into characters of pitiful misfortune. The mayor had cheated them. Disillusioned, having been promised something, having formed ideas in their minds of their futures, of their homes, they saw that yet again they were to be denied the dignity of achievement.

'This is your fault,' Trudie told her brother.

'How?'

'It was you who went to the papers. It was you who made this happen. What gives you the right to choose for everyone? What gives you the right to take houses away from us? We don't care about the past. It's only *now* that we care about.'

'What was I supposed to do? Let him get away with it, let him put us behind a corner, out of sight?'

'You should have let us have houses. You should have forgotten about the stupid *History*.'

The mayor sat in the dark with the curtains drawn, watching the news, his face coming back to him, swollen, livid, through the screen. He felt deceived by what had come to pass. Each morning he had woken knowing that greatness lay ahead of him; that things had been promised to him, by himself, by his own efforts and design. Now he found that everything he had made for himself did not exist. The ability to arrange all things, to bide his time and plan, had come to nothing. There was no substance to what he had done. Nothing had been achieved.

On the morning of the fourth day, the mayor walked out to a grey, cloudless sky. He stood in front of his house, his chin stiff, and spoke to the waiting reporters.

'There is no manuscript,' he said. 'Pieter van Meerman never existed. I made him up. I made up the entire thing. I lied about the houses too. I wanted the upper town gone. I promised them houses so that I could get rid of them.'

It was what they had already known. In fact, many had already written their articles, waiting only for those very words to slot in place before sending them back to their editors. Those words, they knew, would line lamp-posts throughout the country. The reporters began packing up their belongings; by evening none remained, their presence only evident by the litter of polystyrene coffee mugs and cigarette ends which lay outside the mayor's house.

Afterword: Soutbek Today

Present-day Soutbek is a far cry from the small settlement established here in the mid-1660s. Yet that same spirit of generosity and enthusiasm which united such a diverse array of people in the common goal of a better life is in no way absent in the Soutbek of today. Visitors to the town often remark on its 'old-world charm' and 'quiet beauty', as well as the kindness of the locals and its renowned local delicacies. The people in this area live a quiet life, spent mostly in the long-standing industries of fishing and *bokkom*-making. Come to Soutbek on any day of the week and you will be warmly welcomed by the local fishermen and their families. They will gladly take visitors out on their colourful boats, showing them around the rocky coastline, and will allow them to be privy to that self-sufficiency, that independent spirit of the inhabitants which was instilled 350 years ago. The local fishermen still make their nets by hand and it is a truly unique sight to see them sitting on their front doorsteps, mending or constructing nets. With the correct permit (available from the local Post Office) the independence of the Soutbekkers can be replicated by any tourists interested in collecting crayfish or mussels, or even in doing some fishing of their own.

But far from simply remaining quaint and unprogressive, this coastal town has become a favoured holiday destination for national and international tourists alike. Famed for its solitude, Soutbek boasts a wonderful stretch of peaceful coastline, on which one can idle, admire the breathtaking view, whale-watch or simply relax. A protected beach with a tidal pool also makes Soutbek an ideal family destination. Mothers can let their children swim and play without need for concern. For the more active visitor, Soutbek offers a variety of activities such as surfing, horse-riding, hiking and 4x4 trails. It is also a favourite destination of birdwatchers, since the nearby estuary serves as an important habitat for migratory birds, and has recently been registered as an IBA (Important Breeding Area). In addition, Soutbek attracts botanists and nature-lovers from across the globe, owing to the famed riot of colours which erupts each spring in the form of a carpet of flowers that spreads for kilometres. The full beauty of these flowers is best witnessed between the hours of 11:00 and 15:00, the hottest hours of the day, when the blooms turn to face the sun.

No trip to South Africa can be considered complete without first stopping at Soutbek, nor do South Africans any longer have an excuse for not visiting. With its wonderful reputation for professional service and its ability to make everyone feel at home, Soutbek is able to entice even the most exacting tourist. But above all, the mild winters and temperate summers, as well as the peaceful atmosphere, beautiful scenery and a truly rich history, combine to make Soutbek the ideal holiday destination. A destination which, I am sure Pieter van Meerman would agree, it is worth traversing the world to reach.

Pieter Fortuin
Terence Pearson

On the West Coast, winter returned sooner than the previous year. The dry earth of the plains muddied, the grass turned green. In the lower town, those who could had begun to leave. It was not the embarrassment of being associated with Soutbek that drove them away. Rather, it was the continued presence of the homeless in the town hall, the continued stench of litter and human waste. Though they had not been privy to the mayor's plan to resettle the upper towners, they now felt robbed by the lost benefits it would have brought them. A town that was not theirs was no town at all. Houses went on the market or stood empty, their windows crusted over with salt and dust, their gardens overgrown.

Still, despite the emptying town and the lapse of time, the disgrace of his failure kept Pieter indoors. Initially, after his confession, letters had come for him: from his publishers, who were suing him; from his lawyer, notifying him that he was being investigated for fraud, bribery and corruption; and from the town council, informing him that under the circumstances he would be relieved of his position as Mayor of Soutbek. After that he had heard nothing from outside; not from inhabitants of the town, not from further afield.

He stopped washing, stopped dressing. He ate what there was, scrounging in the cupboards for what food still remained. He lived off stale bread; tomato and onion mix eaten straight from the tin; peanut butter. In the freezer he found meat which he placed in the microwave for a few minutes, eating it pink, half-raw. At night he slept in any of the many rooms of his house, dragging a sleeping bag and pillow behind him; afraid to stay in an individual room for two nights running. Sleep punished him. Each night he lay somewhere between sleep and wakefulness, feeling his eyes burning, his skin crawling on his body. Half-dreaming, half-awake he would see the wet form of his father coming towards him holding out a freshly caught fish.

'It is too small,' he would try to tell his father. 'You have to throw it back.'

But his father would not leave, would continue to move towards him, the red flap of his slit throat opening and closing like a gill, until Pieter covered his head with the sleeping bag, gnashing his teeth, begging.

He opened the doors of his liquor cabinet and steadily went through its contents. Too soon the alcohol was gone. It was weeks since he had been outside, weeks since he had spoken to anyone. Drunk, stinking, he made his way outdoors, blinking violently in the dim mid-morning light. It was raining slightly, and cold, but Pieter noticed neither, stumbling down the hill towards the shop, stopping part way in order to check into which pocket he had put his credit card.

He did not pay attention to where he stood. He did not observe the line of glaring faces, did not hear the shouts coming from the soup queue outside the town hall. Only when they began pelting him with hunks of bread and cups of soup did he look up, drawing his arms up to protect his face from the hot liquid. From the queue, from further up the hill, from the town hall, they ran at him. He was confused, stumbling, unable to turn away. They slapped him, kicked him, pushed him to the ground, all the while shouting and cursing. He called out for help, crying out the names of the men who stood guard. But the men were motionless, their faces blank. His body grated on the tar. They kicked and kicked, while he held his arms up in front of his body as though he wasn't there, as though he didn't exist.

From the queue, Charles came forward, calling to the men and women to stop, dragging the mayor away from them. He helped the mayor into his house where he put him on a sofa and brought him some water and a dishcloth to stem the blood.

He made space for himself in a nearby armchair, taking in the squalor of the room. He sighed. 'You can't blame them. I'm not saying it's right, but you can't blame them for how they feel.'

'I know.' He was crying softly.

'And David? Who's looking after him?'

'He's gone. He left. He wants no part of it. I did all of this and he wants no part of it.'

'I'm not questioning why you did it. You had your reasons, I'm sure. I don't know that anyone...'

'You'd do the same for your family, wouldn't you? Your son?'

'Gershwin? Maybe. But what could I give him? He can't go to the high school, he can't get a job. He sits all day, he gives his food to his sisters, I see him.'

'You'd give him a better life if you had the chance.'

'Like what? More food, a job?'

'I don't know anymore. There's nothing left now.'

As the lower town steadily emptied itself of inhabitants, jobs for the upper towners became scarce. With only the small government subsidies that each family received for every child under fifteen, there was not enough to live on. Children ran in the streets. Dogs, too thin to move, lay in the road, panting. The people of the upper town were reduced to frameworks only; to bones and skin. They went to church, they prayed. Their bodies tired, hurting, they kneeled before God, begging for forgiveness for their sins, asking for relief. They spoke of mercy, of salvation, but in their hearts they no longer believed in such things. Leaving the church, they looked up at the large sky coming in black and cold. Around them the wind was strong. They found themselves turning, holding down their hats, their dresses, turning in the wind underneath a black sky; boats on the sea.

Taking advantage of the destitution of the upper towners, a farmer arrived one morning in a large truck. He went from shelter to shelter, explaining that he had a week's work for anyone who was willing. He owned a citrus farm on the banks of the Oliphants River, and would pay R60 a day for *naartjie* pickers, payment at the end of the week. A generous amount, he was careful to observe, for unskilled labourers.

Anna and Sara heard the offer with gratitude. For weeks they had lived on the charity of Willem and his sister, unable to offer anything in return. When the opportunity arose for them to make some money, they readily accepted and were amongst the first to climb on the back of the truck.

At the *naartjie* orchard the farmer gave them a canvas bag apiece, which they were to wear slung over a shoulder. To some he gave stepladders with which to reach the top branches. Anna and Sara walked together through the rows, filling their bags, enjoying the cool air, laughing at their steaming breaths. For six days this routine became their lives. For six days they were fetched before dawn, watching from the back of the truck the world around them slowly unfold as the sun rose; and then in the evening, on the return journey, watching the same objects disappear into night.

On the evening of the sixth day, the farmer waited for everyone to climb out of the truck and made them form a line. Into each waiting hand he placed two R50 notes. Seeing the amount, Sara, who was at the start of the line, stepped forward. 'But where is the rest?'

'What was that, *meisie*?'

'You said R60 a day. That's R360. You still owe us R260 each.'

The farmer smiled. 'Listen *meisie*, you've obviously never done this sort of work before, so let me tell you – I had to meet my expenses. You don't think I'm going to drive all this way twice a day for nothing. That R260 of yours covers your transport every day.'

Sara opened her mouth, ready to say more, but Anna took her by the elbow. 'Come,' she said, 'we need the money.'

Soon the heavy storms came. The river flooded, roads were blocked off. In the upper town they turned to foraging. They stripped the rock pools of mussels and small crabs. They gathered root tubers, winter berries, insects, lizards, the odd mongoose. Some even ate gulls. They no longer recognised themselves by their own faces in the mirror, seeing, instead, their wretchedness in the faces of each other; so that each man and woman became an echo of the next, the original impossible to locate. They squatted in the rubble of their homes, holding in their hands crumbled bricks made by their parents and grandparents. They touched the earth wherever possible; mud and dust and dirt. It was theirs and they carried it with them under their nails, on their skins.

In having the history of Soutbek turned into a lie, to the outside world truth and fiction had now become indistinguishable and the past was a fable, the identities of the inhabitants a mere myth. Robbed of their selves, their ancestors, they were nothing to anyone anymore. In the passing months as hunger and dejection increased, it was as though they had become completely invisible to others. Outside of Soutbek, they no longer existed.

On the packing floors of the fish factory, bodies lay asleep, exhausted. The night was cold; wind blew in from all sides. Somewhere someone was coughing, elsewhere a child whimpered. Out of the dark mass of sleeping forms, a body rose, walking stiffly, unnaturally, as though entirely made of bone. It limped through the sleepers, careful not to wake anyone. Exiting the factory floor, it walked out to the land, littered and foul beside the jetty. There, in the moonlight, the shape came out of the shadow and the face was clear: young, tired, hardly yet a man. The tide was low and he waded awkwardly out towards the far end of the jetty which still stood. At the upright, he pulled himself stiffly up the ragged sides, resting on the shit-covered concrete at the top, leaning against the crane which still remained. He sat and looked out at the sea, dark, still, endless before him. Behind him the land was quiet, expanding out and out.

The following morning they saw his body, hanging from the crane, a noose made from shoelaces. The tide was in and it was hours before anyone could get to him to take him down.

The mayor did not recognise Anna when he arrived at the Cupido house, foul, unable to stand. She was small, too thin, her face lined and drawn.

'Sit down,' she said. 'I'll get you some water.'

'Some food. I need food,' he replied.

'There is none.'

'Nothing?'

'Nothing.'

'Water then.'

She knelt down beside him, holding a cup to his lips, and he drank loudly. He put his hand up, tried to touch her arm, but she moved away, wrinkling her nose at the stench of him. After the beating at the soup kitchen, he had not left the house during the day. Only at night did he go outside, scrabbling through the rubbish bins of those few remaining inhabitants of the lower town. He was sick; he had broken ribs, a broken nose. He lived on bread crusts and chicken bones.

'I didn't want this,' he said.

Anna said nothing.

'I wanted to feel proud,' he belched quietly, wiping his mouth with his sleeve. Anna held the chipped cup to his lips again. His head tipped back, and he lay where he was, breathing deeply, slowly.

He woke to the sound of hymns being sung. He was cold, lying on a concrete floor. He got up unsteadily, coughing up phlegm and clutching at his ribs. Outside the singing continued, and he left the house, following the sound. Near the church he stopped, seeing a large crowd in the graveyard. It was a funeral, for the suicide. There had been no objection from the congregation to burying Gershwin Geduld in the cemetery. They knew what had killed him, they knew that that same thing existed inside each of their own bodies.

Six men had dug the grave, taking hours, as the wet soil kept caving in. Into this crumbling pit they lowered the body. There was no coffin, only a sheet to hold the corpse, lowered down by means of two ropes held by four men.

From where he stood, he looked out at the shacks around him, at the people assembled around the grave. Beyond the cemetery, in the distance, the cargo train was moving in an endless line towards the further coast. When the last of the carriages was out of sight, he turned, walking away from the upper town, the hill, the beach, away from Soutbek and his house, with its many rooms, empty.

Glossary of South African terms and phrases

Baas: master; sir: term of address used by a black or coloured person in South Africa to address a white man. This type of address is now discouraged, but still continues, particularly in farming and rural communities.

Bakkie: a small truck with an open body and low sides; from Afrikaans *bak* meaning 'container'.

Bokkom: dried, salted fish – popular on the west coast.

Buchu: shrub common in South Africa. Latin names: *Barosma betulina, Barosma serratifolia, Barosma crenulata.* Used for medicinal purposes as an antiseptic and to treat the common cold, upset stomachs, urinary tract infections, gout, rheumatism, yeast infections, and many more.

Dagga: cannabis.

Doek: a square of cloth or a scarf worn mainly to cover the head.

Dop: a tot or a drink of alcohol.

Dronkgat: drunk arsehole.

'Ek's die Queen van Genot!'… 'Ou Queenie, ja! Wys o's Queenie!': 'I'm the Queen of Genot!' … 'Old Queenie, yes! Show us Queenie!'

Kleinbaasie: young or small master (see 'Baas').

Kraal: enclosure for cattle or sheep.

Meisie: girl – in this case used in a derogatory fashion.

Naartjie: a soft, loose-skinned South African citrus fruit. It is similar to the mandarin, satsuma or tangerine.

Nikswerd: worthless.

Oom: uncle.

Plaaswag: like a neighbourhood watch, but consists of armed farmers in farming areas protecting their lands.

Suurvye: sour fig plant.

Veld: open grass- and scrubland.

ACKNOWLEDGEMENTS

While the events, characters and many of the places in this novel are fictional, much of the inspiration for this work was drawn from several trips to the West Coast towns of Strandfontein and Doringbaai between February 2008 and February 2009. At all times I have been careful to remember that though this is a work of fiction, it is a tale nonetheless which represents a sore reality, and I have tried my utmost to relate it in a sympathetic and sensitive manner. However, if this is not evident, then the failure is all mine, and I apologise sincerely.

There are a number of people I would like to thank for their kindness to me during the time spent in the writing of this novel.

Firstly, I would like to thank the National Arts Council of South Africa for making it possible through financial assistance for me to write uninterruptedly for six months, thus producing the first draft of *Finding Soutbek*. Furthermore, I want to thank my parents, Keith and Esmarie Jennings; Carla Potgieter; Johan and Linnea Potgieter; Megan Witbooi of 'Die Hawe', Doringbaai's community centre; the learners of Voortrekker High and Fish Hoek Senior High Schools who so kindly donated bags and bags of toys, school supplies and clothing to the Doringbaai Community Centre; Damon Galgut; Carrol Clarkson; Tannie Babs Conradie; Carlo Germeshuys Snr and Sandra Germeshuys; Jean Keiser; Lesley Marx; Fedde van den Bosch for translations of the more difficult, archaic Dutch; Colleen Higgs; Liesl Jobson and Pieter van Eede

Most of all I must thank Carlo Germeshuys Jnr. No part of this novel would be possible without him, and each page is a testament to his extraordinary faith in me.

Karen Jennings, Cape Town, July 2011

BIBLIOGRAPHY

Anthonisz, Jan, *Dagh Register Gehouden by den Oppercoopman Deel III 1659–1662*, eds D.B. Bosman and H.B. Thom, Kaapstad: A.A. Balkema: Uitgawe van die Van Riebeeck-vereniging, 1957.

Böeseken, A.J., 'Die Koms van die Blankes onder Van Riebeeck,' *Vyfhonderd Jaar Suid-Afrikaanse Geskiedenis*, ed. C.F.J. Muller, Pretoria & Kaapstad: Academica, 1968, pp. 17–27.

—'Die Vestiging van die Blankes onder die Van der Stels,' *Vyfhonderd Jaar Suid-Afrikaanse Geskiedenis*, ed. C.F.J. Muller, Pretoria & Kaapstad: Academica, 1968, pp. 27–40.

—'Die Geheime Bekoring van Afrika,' *Vyfhonderd Jaar Suid-Afrikaanse Geskiedenis*, ed. C.F.J. Muller, Pretoria & Kaapstad: Academica, 1968, pp. 40–51.

Burman, Jose, *Who Really Discovered South Africa?*, Cape Town: Struik, 1969.

Conradie, Elizabeth, *Hollandse skrywers uit Suid-Afrika. 'n Kultuur-historiese studie. Deel I (1652-1875)*, Pretoria: J.H. de Bussy & Kaapstad: H.A.U.M. v/h J. Dusseau, 1934.

Elphick, Richard, *Khoikhoi and the Founding of White South Africa*, Johannesburg: Ravan Press, 1985.

Foster, Ronel, 'Die Boekstawing van die Sewentiende-eeuse Landsreise. Die Omsetting van Gebeurtenis tot Feit,' *Tydskrif vir Nederlands & Afrikaans* 11.1 (Junie 2004), 10 October 2008: http://academic.sun.ac.za/afrndl/tna/foster04.html

Grutter, Wilhelm and D.J. van Zyl, *The Story of South Africa*, Cape Town, Pretoria, Johannesburg: Human and Rousseau, 1981.

Hahn, Theophilus, *Tsuni-//goam, the Supreme Being of the Khoikhoi*, London: Trubner and Co., 1881.

Hoernle, A. Winifred, 'The Social Organization of the Namaqua Hottentots of Southwest Africa,' *American Anthropologist* 27.1 (1925), pp. 1–24.

Huigen, Siegfried, *De weg naar Monomotapa. Nederlandstalige representaties van geografische, historische en sociale werkelijkheden in Zuid-Afrika*, Amsterdam: Amsterdam University Press, 1996.

Kostka, Berit, 'Namaqualand – A Short History of Nearly Everything,' *FSM (Four Striped Mouse) Times* 4 (July–September 2005), pp. 8–17.

Mountain, Alan, *The First People of the Cape*, Cape Town: David Philip, 2003.

Schapera, I, *The Khoisan Peoples of South Africa: Bushmen and Hottentots*, London: Routledge and Kegan Paul Ltd, 1930.

Scholtz, Philippus Lodewikus, 'Die Historiese Ontwikkeling van die Onder-Olifantsrivier 1660–1902,' *Argief-jaarboek vir Suid-Afrikaanse Geskiedenis*, ed. A. Keiser et al., Kaapstad: Die publikasie afdeling van die Kantoor van die Direkteur van Argiewe, 1966, pp. 1–212.

Smith, Andy et al., *The Bushmen of Southern Africa: A Foraging Society in Transition,*. Cape Town: David Philip Publishers, 2000.

Tribe, Geoff, 'Meerhoff's Casteel en route to Monomotapa,' *Village Life* No. 32 (Oct/Nov 2008), pp. 40–45.

Van Riebeeck, Jan, *Journal of Jan van Riebeeck Volume One*, ed. H.B. Thom, Cape Town: Balkema, 1958.

Webley, L., 'Archaeological evidence for pastoralist land-use and settlement in Namaqualand over the last 2000 years,' *Journal of Arid Environments* 70 (2007), pp. 629–640.

THE AUTHOR

Karen Jennings was born in Cape Town in 1982. She holds Master's degrees in both English Literature and Creative Writing from the University of Cape Town.

Karen's stories and poetry have been published in journals across the globe, in countries as diverse as Nigeria, Australia and Greece. In 2010 her short story *From Dark* won the Africa Region prize in the Commonwealth Short Story Competition. *Mia and the Shark* won the English section of the Maskew Miller Longman short story competition in 2009 and is now studied in schools. *Finding Soutbek* is her first novel.

Karen is currently researching her second novel as part of a PhD in Creative Writing at the University of KwaZulu-Natal under the supervision of Kobus Moolman.

More details are available from
www.hollandparkpress.co.uk/jennings

Holland Park Press is a unique publishing initiative. It gives contemporary Dutch writers the opportunity to be published in Dutch and English. We also publish new works written in English and translations of classic Dutch novels.

To

- Find out more
- Learn more about Karen Jennings
- Discover other interesting books
- Read our unique Anglo-Dutch magazine
- Practice your writing skills
- Take part in discussions
- Or just make a comment

Visit www.hollandparkpress.co.uk